ALSO BY ANDRÉ ACIMAN

## Fiction
*Find Me*
*Enigma Variations*
*Harvard Square*
*Eight White Nights*
*Call Me by Your Name*

## Nonfiction
*Roman Year: A Memoir*
*Homo Irrealis: The Would-Be Man Who Might Have Been*
*Roman Hours* (with Jeannette Montgomery Barron)
*Alibis: Essays on Elsewhere*
*The Light of New York* (with Jean-Michel Berts)
*Entrez: Signs of France* (with Steven Rothfeld)
*False Papers: Essays on Exile and Memory*
*Out of Egypt: A Memoir*

## As Editor
*The Proust Project*
*Letters of Transit: Reflections on Exile, Identity,
Language, and Loss*

# ROOM

## ON THE

# SEA

# ROOM
## ON THE
# SEA

**THREE NOVELLAS**

# ANDRÉ
# ACIMAN

**FARRAR, STRAUS AND GIROUX**
**NEW YORK**

Farrar, Straus and Giroux
120 Broadway, New York 10271

EU Representative: Macmillan Publishers Ireland Ltd, 1st Floor,
The Liffey Trust Centre, 117–126 Sheriff Street Upper,
Dublin 1, DO1 YC43

Library of Congress Cataloging-in-Publication Data
Names: Aciman, André, author. | Aciman, André.
Gentleman from Peru. | Aciman, André. Room on the sea. |
Aciman, André. Mariana.
Title: Room on the sea : three novellas / André Aciman.
Other titles: Room on the sea (Compilation)
Description: First edition. | New York : Farrar, Straus and
Giroux, 2025.
Identifiers: LCCN 2024053325 | ISBN 9780374613419 (hardcover)
Subjects: LCGFT: Novels.
Classification: LCC PS3601.C525 R66 2025 | DDC 813/.6—
dc23/eng/20241206
LC record available at https://lccn.loc.gov/2024053325

Our books may be purchased in bulk for promotional, educational,
or business use. Please contact your local bookseller or the
Macmillan Corporate and Premium Sales Department at
1-800-221-7945, extension 5442, or by email at
MacmillanSpecialMarkets@macmillan.com.

www.fsgbooks.com
Follow us on social media at @fsgbooks

10 9 8 7 6 5 4 3 2 1

*For*

*Rebecca Hartje,*

*Mollye Shacklette,*

*and*

*Hemin Shin*

# CONTENTS

# THE GENTLEMAN FROM PERU

## Chapter One

"Perhaps this might help," said the stranger. He walked over to their table and touched Mark on the shoulder. "Just breathe deeply and count to five." They'd been seeing him for at least three days, sitting across from them at a corner table in the hotel's dining area by the pool. Always keeping to himself, occasionally exchanging a few short pleasantries with the tall, white-haired waiter, otherwise very quiet and reserved.

Though he always sat alone, he never brought anything to read with him—just a green Moleskine notebook, which he kept open upside down like a diminutive camping tent; a tiny black, clipless fountain pen; and a pair of glasses, which he tossed on the table with total disregard for how they landed on the tablecloth, as though still denying that he needed them. He was in his early sixties, and looked dapper, slim, and always buoyant in his well-pressed double-breasted navy seersucker jacket, linen shirt, and silver-gray tie, topped by a vibrant-colored pocket square.

They had spotted him a few times in the lobby or on the long terrace and had begun wondering about him,

probably thinking he was another one of those stereo-
typical semi-retired Italian gentlemen who'd done well
for themselves and who pick a spa in the hills or a beach
resort where they vacation, socialize a bit, play bridge at
night, and for a few weeks manage to stay away from
their wives, mistresses, and grandchildren. But this gentleman didn't socialize, didn't play bridge, hadn't come for
the waters or the mud baths, and unlike the other hotel
guests, kept asking the waiters to lower the volume of
the already muted Vivaldi music piped into the dining
area. Once, on heading to what was usually his table,
he had thrown a glance in their direction, even given
them an imperceptible bow as a passing salutation, but
he never uttered a word. They did not return his greeting, feeling that his old-world manner was too chilly
and formal for them to know exactly how to respond.
Their eyes had simply cast a blank, bewildered stare on
his figure, ignoring his distant salutation and trying not
to encourage what he might be up to next. "I'm telling
you, he's been studying us," said one of them. "Weird,"
agreed another.

Their table was the busiest and largest in the hotel
dining area and occupied the space lining a good por-
tion of the balustrade overlooking the beach and the ma-
rina on the left. As soon as they'd shown up the first
few times, the waiters had hastily joined together three
tables and thrown a long tablecloth over them. Later, after they'd all finished eating and left, the waiters would
remove the long tablecloth, crumple it up, and separate
the tables again. Eventually, seeing that the cohort never
went elsewhere for breakfast or dinner, the waiters decided to leave the tables joined together for the remainder of their stay. They were not the only Americans in

the hotel, but the youngest and the loudest. When the two guitarists came round to their table in the evening, the women in their group would suddenly beam, turn to face the players, and laugh as they attempted to hum along with the music. Everyone else in the hotel spoke softly, ate very slowly, and drank far less. The young Americans were the last to leave at night, and, by the time they'd ordered dessert, all the other tables were already being set up for breakfast.

After dinner, most of the aging hotel guests liked to spend their time either lounging in the common area not far from the lobby or playing bridge in the card room. For them, this was not a resort where you came for a few days but where you spent at least three weeks in the hotel and stayed there, socializing with other guests who'd been coming here for years if not decades, and touring the environs a bit only to return for a short swim, then light cocktails and a splendid dinner. The chef, as the hotel staff kept reminding the young *signori Americani*, was world famous and the author of three bestselling cookbooks. After dinner, the much older folk would sip mineral water or chamomile on the veranda or, fearing drafts, would eventually repair to the tearoom. They were dubbed "the knitting pool" by the young Americans, because two of the eldest women were frequently seen knitting, while the men, who later seemed eager to move to the patio to discuss the sorry state of Italian politics, would sit in groups of three and four before turning in when it got a tad chilly. After dinner, the young Americans liked to crowd into the small bar area that probably housed more gins and single malts than any luxury bar in the United Kingdom.

"I wonder if the ladies play gin rummy after napping

in the afternoon," said Margot, one of the Americans, who worked in an art gallery and was seldom reluctant to crack a snarky remark about people she didn't know. Everyone laughed. "Yes, but do you know what happens to their husbands?" asked Oscar, who was a Chilean schooled in the United States and had a savage sense of humor. He waited awhile for someone to hazard an answer, and seeing no one did, he couldn't help but elicit the old joke about why such husbands invariably died first. "Why do they die first?" asked Margot, yanking off his sailor's cap and dropping it on her head. "Because they want to die," he answered.

The group burst out laughing again. Margot stared at the two eldest ladies, who had been discussing knitting stitches, and smiled a vague, long-distance smile at them. "Just promise to shoot me if I end up knitting in a hotel drinking overheated chamomile when I am eighty." And with this she gave Oscar his sailor's cap again but, to tease him, tilted the visor to his left. He readjusted the cap, but she struggled to turn its visor to his right this time. "Old people live way too long," she said, letting go of the hat.

The two pensioners didn't know they were the butt of so much humor, and, catching smiles on the young Americans from across the dining area, exchanged subdued nods that could easily pass for an unspoken greeting. "They're waking up," said Margot. "Mustn't rouse the old ducks." "You're being mean again," said Mark, who was the voice of reason in the group.

Margot caught herself, was quiet at first, then, staring straight back at him, said, "I know." But seeing no one had said anything, she added, "I was just thinking of my grandmother who was lucky enough to die in her sleep. I want to be spared getting old."

"Still," Mark continued, "you shouldn't say things like that. I lost my grandma a few weeks ago, and I loved her." Mark always wore one piece of tennis gear or another even when he wasn't playing. Now, because of a recent injury, he was continually rubbing his shoulder.

The well-dressed gentleman, however, stood out from everyone else in the hotel and seemed perfectly content to be left alone. Paul, who worked in DC for a congressman, had run into the man in the airy hotel lobby and, without knowing why, had greeted him with a noncommittal smile that he couldn't retract in time. The gentleman had made a perfunctory nod but hadn't smiled. "He just hates us," said Mark.

"Could be a hired assassin type living off the fat of his Swiss bank account," said Margot.

"No, an assassin on his last job."

"Who is he killing?"

"Maybe one of us," said Paul.

"I see him as a painter," said Angelica, who always came to the dining area already wearing a bathing suit and a translucent wraparound.

"Maybe."

"He's too old-school to be an artist."

"Gives me the heebie-jeebies," said Margot.

After breakfast the gentleman would leave as quietly as he had entered. "Probably meeting his mole."

"Mossad."

"Why Mossad?"

"Looks Jewish and far too slick for someone born into wealth. There's something fishy about him."

"You're being mean again, Margot."

After dinner the gentleman liked to sit on the veranda by himself and smoke a cigarette, sometimes two.

On their third night they watched him do something totally unusual. He had gone back inside, changed into his bathing suit, and walked down the stairs leading to the beach, where he started swimming all alone in the dark. The Americans never saw him come back up the stairs.

"I can just see it in the papers: *Ex-assassin takes his own life.*"

"Stop it already."

"I wonder what his deal is."

They agreed that none of them understood him. But then they never gave him much thought and inevitably forgot about him. All they seemed to care about was enjoying the hotel and the surrounding beach. By daylight they liked to go swimming and boating; they spent long hours at breakfast, lunch, and dinner, and in the evening, after a stint at the hotel bar, they liked to go partying at one of the various nightclubs around the hills.

At first, no one could tell why he had walked over to their table or why he was aiming straight for Mark. But before anyone knew what was happening, he had placed his palm on Mark's right shoulder; he did not apologize for intruding, did not ask permission, didn't even hesitate to make what was clearly an invasive gesture. Instead, he spoke his few words with the effortless ease and authority of someone who'd done it many times before. "Perhaps this might help," he said.

Stunned by the move, everyone at their table gaped as the gentleman, who was diminutive by comparison to the athlete, said, "No, don't move yet, just give it a few seconds." And then immediately started the countdown "Five, four, three, two, one"—after which he slowly removed his hand. "The pain should be gone now."

Mark, whose shoulder was quite sore since his tennis injury, was so startled by the appearance of the white-bearded stranger in the navy-blue sports jacket that he did not know how to react or what to say. But moments later, "I can't believe it," he said, standing up. Everyone thought he was about to shove the stranger aside or hit him across the face. Instead, he reached for his right shoulder with his left hand, and kept groping the area around it as if trying to see whether the pain had indeed vanished or moved elsewhere. "I can't feel any pain, it's just not there," he repeated with total disbelief. He continued to twist himself around to check his neck, his back, the back of his skull, still trying to determine how the pain, which had been crippling him for days, had slipped away in a matter of seconds simply because the stranger in the navy jacket had taken the liberty of placing a hand on his shoulder and counted down the seconds.

"But where did the pain go?" he asked, turning to his friends, as though they'd know any more than he did. He was still startled and kept looking around and behind him as though someone had filched his wallet and was about to toss it over to another guest as a practical joke. For a moment he seemed to be asking the man who had healed him to put the pain back where it belonged.

But the pain wasn't there.

"Pain's like a sneaky reptile," said the stranger. "It appears on its own, inhabits your body for as long as it chooses, sometimes forever, and if you're lucky, it sneaks away without saying goodbye."

For a moment it seemed to Mark that he was being used as an unwitting prop in a party trick. Someone pretends to guess the card you picked, but you know it's a trick. He'll saw a woman in two, but you've seen it done many times. He pulls coins from behind your ear and you laugh like a three-year-old, though you know it's a sham. Sometimes someone will hypnotize you and make you say things in public you wouldn't dare whisper to yourself, but all along you know it's bogus. On a rare occasion a magician will explain his trick to his public, and just when everyone thinks they got it and can't wait to perform it on someone else, lo and behold, the explanation turns out to be a party trick as well—and you're no wiser than you were at the beginning of the show.

But this was real. As the man said: the pain didn't even bother saying goodbye. "So, it's like gone, gone?" Mark asked. "Or will I find it at the count of three?"

The stranger looked at him with a patronizing smile the way Jesus might have looked at Lazarus after raising him from the dead, meaning *Have faith, brother, you're good to go.*

"And I can throw away all the meds everyone made me buy these past few weeks?"

"You can flush them down the toilet," the stranger said, with a hint of a snicker in his voice. "You'll be fine, trust me."

"And you do this for . . . free?" Mark asked, already worried at being presented with a bill.

"Totally for free," echoed the gentleman. "On the house."

"No second visit?" Mark finally asked, meaning to inject humor so as not to look totally humbled by the experience.

"No second visit."

"So, this is it, then?" an incredulous Mark continued.

"This is it."

"Seriously?"

The older man looked at Mark with quizzical eyes. "Look, I'm no soapbox huckster and this was not a magic show," he finally said in flawless Oxonian English that bore the faintest trace of a Hispanic accent. "It was obvious from my table that you were in pain, I could see you writhing and stiffening, and I wanted to make it go away. That's all. I promise."

Sensing the heavy silence that had fallen between them, the stranger seemed about to click his heels, withdraw, and go back to his table when Mark invited him to join them for a glass of wine and dessert. He had meant to add a few words of thanks, but the stranger hushed him with a gesture and simply said "With pleasure" to the invitation. They squeezed together to make room for an extra chair, which the tall waiter brought to their table. "It will be my second glass of wine and dessert. I try not to have more than one a day." He asked them what had brought them to this place.

The question made almost all of them laugh, as they looked around the table to see who was going to tell their story. "We were invited," said Basil, a lawyer in a large firm specializing in mergers, "by a friend who rented the boat we sailed on. But at the last minute he had to stay in New York and wasn't able to come with us to Lisbon. So the boat picked us up in Lisbon and we've been sailing since, hoping to meet up with him at some point."

"But why here?" asked the stranger.

"Apparently there's engine trouble, which is why we

had to stop. The mechanics said they are working on repairs, but frankly, being here, in this hotel, with this beach and everything paid for, is beyond amazing. I, for one, don't care how long the repairs take."

"Agreed," said Emma. "Engine trouble or not, I'm seriously tempted to unpack my things, settle here, and live the rest of my life with my paintbrushes, canvases, and beautiful views and be far away from New York and every male of our species." Then, after a pause, she said, "I'm Emma."

"You look like such fast friends on a splendid private cruise." He envied their camaraderie, he said.

"Well, we all graduated from college ten years ago. We made a vow."

"What vow?"

"That the first to get rich would rent a boat and invite the others on a cruise. None of us made millions, but Malcolm did, and he made good on his promise."

"Except he isn't with you because of work."

"Except he isn't with us because of work," repeated Angelica, with a wry inflection in her voice as if reproaching Malcolm for being far too devoted to his millions when there were other, better things in life. "But tell us who you are," she asked.

"My name is Raúl." A round of introductions and handshakes followed. Mark, Basil, Emma, Claire, Angelica, Paul, Margot, and Oscar. They were eight at their table, so Basil was sure that Raúl wouldn't remember their names. But Raúl shook hands with everyone with a show of paying attention to each name. How long had he been staying here? Mark asked. Ten days. Where was he from? Originally, Peru, but he had studied in England and France as well as in the United States. Was this his first time here? No. He'd been coming here almost every summer since his earliest childhood. He still owned a house on the hill but never slept there, as it was leased to a family friend. Where was he off to next? Back to France, he told them. "But I'm somewhat attached to this place," he explained.

"Somewhat attached?" quipped Margot, using his very own words. "What does that mean, exactly? Either you are or aren't attached to it."

Raúl turned to her and smiled broadly, almost amused at the gratuitous dig. "I suppose more attached to it than I might care to claim." He didn't seem to mind being riled, and Margot had a mirthful way about her that could pry open stuck doors.

"Why more attached than you might care to claim?" asked a perplexed Margot, who repeated his words but, hearing vagueness in what the man said, was pouncing on every opportunity to get him to say what he meant.

"Don't pay attention to her manner," interrupted Emma. "She can't rein it in once she starts. She's just playing with you."

"I like that. It might make me tell more than I normally like to tell a perfect stranger."

"I'm not perfect," Margot snapped. "Anyone will tell you that."

He looked at her, smiled once more, said nothing at first, then quietly added, "But you are perfect. And you know it too. Though you may be wrong about one thing."

"How so?"

"You're not a stranger." By the sudden expression on her face, he must have sensed that his words had baffled her.

"So, why aren't we strangers?" she asked with a nervous, undecided smile. She was, as her expression suggested, giving him all the rope he needed to hang himself. "You've been watching us for days now. So, obviously, you might know a few things about us."

"That's not why we aren't strangers."

Margot's shoulders stiffened. "So, let's hear it," she said, staring at him with a goading smile.

"You two are having fun, I can tell," said Oscar. "When was the last time we saw Margot smile?"

"She never smiles," said Mark.

"I wasn't smiling," she protested.

There was a pause. The gentleman asked for a second glass of wine. "It will be my third," he said, almost as though admitting to a weakness. "A terrible precedent." Then, after a pause: "Your name is Marya."

"My name is Margot." She was snapping at him now.

"Yes, but I could have sworn Marya was your birth name."

"Why?"

"If you ask it's because you already know the answer."

She looked at him with rising displeasure, as if deciding to contain her temper. "My mother had wanted to name me Marya, but my father wanted Margaret, so they settled on Margot. But nobody knows this. How could you possibly have known—did you know her, did you know my mother?" She sounded angry, as though ready to go to battle.

"I know many things about all of you."

"Oh? Name some!" said Margot.

"I will tell you. But on one condition. First, may I have a slice of the cassata? It's very good, which is why I never order it."

Basil signaled to the waiter.

"So, what is it that you know?" Margot asked.

Raúl took a hasty sip from his glass. This is when, turning to Mark and holding the refilled wineglass lightly between two fingers, he uttered one word only: "Twenty-two."

Mark looked at him quizzically. "What about twenty-two?" he asked.

"You know exactly," replied Raúl.

Mark had no idea what. But then it hit him. "You looked me up at the front desk!" he exclaimed.

"No, I didn't. But it is January twenty-second, isn't it?"

Mark looked around the table and began to feel as hollow and transparent as the near-emptied bottle of wine standing in the glass bucket next to him. But for his shoulder he would have dismissed the whole thing. He didn't believe in the supernatural, couldn't stand anyone who did, and the air of uplifted piety of those who speak of auras and astral houses brought out the worst in him. Now he was no longer sure.

Raúl looked around the table. "I can tell, for example, that you were born in May," he said to Claire. "And the two of you were born in August," he told Angelica and Paul, "which says a lot. And you," he said, turning to Basil, "are November."

Silence. He told the remaining two sitting at the table the month of their birth. No one disagreed.

"You left me out," said Margot.

"I know."

"Well?"

"You were born in a leap year, were you not?" he said, turning to Margot. "Do you like twenty-eighth of February or first of March? Your pick."

She looked totally dumbstruck.

"Let's drink to that," said Basil, turning to the waiter, who had just opened another bottle to replace the one in the bucket.

"You looked us up online," said Basil. "The easiest trick in the book."

"No, I didn't," said the gentleman from Peru. "So let me turn to you, Basil," he added with a tone that had lost all humor. "You had a twin brother but he died in utero, and by the time you were born there wasn't a trace of him left."

"This is total nonsense," said Basil, trying to contain himself and remain cordial with the gentleman. Then, with a glint of irony on his features: "Are you suggesting I cannibalized my twin brother?"

"Happens more often than you think."

"This is totally freaky," said Mark.

"If you don't believe me, please text your mother in New Orleans right now and ask if she had expected twins."

"How did you know she lives in New Orleans?"

Without looking at Basil, Raúl simply stared at his empty glass and said, "I just know."

"How could you possibly know about twins?" asked Basil. "Did you have access to hospital records? Unless you knew my mother, or her gynecologist, or whatever."

"I don't like rummaging into family secrets. So, let's stay with the missing twin," said Raúl.

Meanwhile, Basil had taken out his phone and began texting the question to his mother. "We'll see what she says," he said, still shaking his head at the absurdity of the question.

"I already know what she'll say," said Raúl.

"Oh, don't listen to him," said Margot, fidgeting in her seat and looking more vexed by the minute. "This whole thing is one big hoax, Basil. He looked us up online. He's probably the hotel magician, hustler, and con artist who comes with breakfast, free Wi-Fi, and cable TV." She looked at Mark. "Was the shoulder cure a hoax as well?"

"Well, maybe it's a placebo effect," interjected Mark, "but, to be honest, the pain did go away."

"If you believe I'm a swindler, let me be more specific." And turning to Emma, Raúl said: "You lost someone two months ago."

"I did."

"You'd borrowed but never returned his watch."

"Yes."

"The reversible watch with the blue face."

"That's correct."

"And the man was your father."

Totally stunned, Emma sat still. Her chin was quivering and she was clearly on the verge of tears. "I kept it because I knew he was dying and I didn't want it left in the house with all the visiting nurses around. In my absurd moments, I kept hoping to return it to him if he got better. But how do you know all this?"

"I'll explain later. But I couldn't have looked it up, could I?" he said, turning to Margot, who seemed even more flustered as she leaned forward, looked around the table, and finally stood up, saying, "I think I'll go for a walk."

Raúl raised his head and looked at her. "Don't go yet. Please."

She did not reply and simply rammed her chair back to the table. It made a loud noise. But then she stood bolted to the spot.

Meanwhile, "Here it is," said Basil, who had just that moment received a text from his mother in New Orleans.

"And what does your mother say?" asked Margot.

Basil stared at Raúl. "You were right. Apparently, they had suspected twins but only one child was born. But my mother asked how I knew this, and honestly, I don't know what to tell her."

"Tell her nothing."

"This is becoming really ugly," exclaimed Margot, and, in a huff, she stormed out of the dining area.

"I think I must have upset her," said Raúl as he turned, looking surprised. "With Margot, one never knows.

"So, I'll enjoy this last drop of wine and head back to my room," he added. Yet he was staring at Angelica and Paul. "You are not married, are you?"

Paul seemed startled by the question, and hesitated before answering. "I'm not. She is. I thought you knew everything," came his little dig.

"Here is what I do know. You two were in love in college, weren't you? Yet neither of you ever did anything about it. No one knew. You yourselves didn't know, or didn't want to know, and have been struggling not to know it ever since, even now, among your friends at this very table. Am I right so far?"

Paul looked over at Angelica, smiled uneasily, and said, "He may have a point."

Angelica did not respond right away. "Could be," she finally said, but was quiet again, and then, speaking softly and smiling awkwardly as if trying to make light of what had just been said: "Do you think Raúl's onto us, just maybe, maybe?"

"Why, have I spoken out of turn?" asked a baffled Raúl.

"Nah. We've known for years," intervened Basil. "Everyone here suspected. How long did it take for this to come out?"

"Just ten years," said a humbled Paul.

"Feels like fifty to us," said Oscar, laughing.

"Actually," said Raúl, "it took three centuries."

"Any more stunning revelations in your bag of tricks, old man?" asked Oscar.

Raúl did not say anything. He just stood up. "Enough magic for one round," he said, and politely pushed back his seat.

## Chapter Two

The next evening the group of young Americans walked into the dining area just about when everyone else in the hotel was finishing dessert. Raúl, as always, was starting his second course by himself. As soon as the Americans spotted him, they greeted him. Mark even patted him on the back with a jovial, hail-fellow, semi-patronizing gesture meant both to express his abiding gratitude and to erase the pitiable figure he must have cut the day before as the injured athlete of the group. They asked if he would like to join them for drinks at the hotel bar after he was done with dinner. "With pleasure," replied the gentleman from Peru.

They had planned on going to one of the clubs around the hill, but had eventually decided to stay put on the hotel grounds. "You'll be our guest. Or, rather, Malcolm's guest. We've told him about you—he's sorry he couldn't be here to meet you."

Raúl gave the invitation to the bar table some thought, almost as though he regretted having accepted so readily and should have reconsidered. Then he added: "Tell Malcolm to beware of any last-minute transaction before the markets close today. He may not be able to avert or reverse its course, but he can certainly take provisions by hedging against the risks. Don't forget."

Basil made an it's-been-duly-noted gesture, but Raúl, pointing his fork at him, insisted: "Tell him now, as in this minute."

"Now, as in now?"

"Exactly," said Raúl. "Call him!

"He's involved in crazy ventures," Raúl explained to those around him, "but I know that this one is dangerous and he needs to sell before the markets close today."

The call was made. It lasted no more than a few seconds. Angelica grabbed the phone and told him she missed him. He missed her too.

"Malcolm thanks you," she told Raúl a moment later.

Later in the evening, as they gathered in the tiny bar and ordered drinks, Mark remarked that if Raúl was so good at forecasting volatile shifts in the market, why hadn't his skills helped him make a fortune himself?

"Because I know nothing about the markets. Besides, I'm always afraid of risking the funds my good parents left me. I often know what dangers lie in store or what people are planning or plotting to do. But I've been tragically blind in the past—the greatest catastrophe in my life caught me totally by surprise. There've been other, terrible instances where my predictions simply proved totally wrong. But birthdays and past events are not difficult for me. Still, I know something is afoot in New York today. You watch: something will happen just before the market closes in half an hour."

As they were relishing their drinks, Raúl told them he'd take them to see something special in the coming days if they had nothing better to do. Had any of them read the *Aeneid*?

Many of them had read bits and pieces. "Courtesy of our liberal arts education, which cost our parents a fortune," said Oscar, "and yet it all boils down to bits and pieces. Which is why we know nothing."

"Exactly," said Margot.

"They taught us contemporary poetry and contemporary issues, even contemporary grammar. But ultimately, like Margot says, nothing," said Oscar.

"*Like* Margot says?" she asked, making fun of him.

"*As* Margot says. *Apologizomai.*"

Everyone laughed. "Courtesy of college Greek 101." All toasted their alma mater.

Raúl didn't quite understand why they were laughing but let the matter pass. He simply added that, if they wanted, he would take them to where Cuma was, one of the spots where Aeneas stopped on his travels after leaving Carthage. There, incidentally, lies the entrance to Avernus, the doorway to the world of the dead, on Lake Avernus.

"Have you been there?" asked Margot.

"Yes. But never alone."

"Why? I'd like to go," said Paul.

"Me too," said Angelica.

"It's the kind of thing Fellini would have loved, a group of friends working their way down a craggy passage into the underworld where we're told Styx, the sacred river, ran. There you'll see the mourning fields, the *Lugentes campi*," explained Raúl. "This is where all broken hearts tell their woebegone tales of love to anyone who passes by and cares to listen: Phaedra, who took her own life for loving her stepson after she opened up her heart to him; Dido, who lit a fire and threw herself into it while Aeneas watched her burn from aboard his ship to Italy; Procris, who was mistakenly speared by her lover; and poor Caenis, raped by a god and begging to be turned into a man so as never to be raped again. Haven't you all been burnt and speared and raped in your hearts at least once?"

"No comment," said Oscar, which made everyone burst out laughing. But no one answered.

"Which means all of you have," said Raúl.

"Everyone's been hurt. But I still can't believe that people actually take their own lives for love. It's so kitsch, so camp."

That was Margot.

"I almost did once. At least I thought of it very, very seriously," said Emma. "But I wasn't going to do it with violence or with pills, so I decided to starve myself. And I almost did. Then one day I saw someone eating country bread with triple-cream cheese and drinking a glass of red, and I said: *Enough!*"

"It would be just like Emma to be saved by cheese," said Oscar.

"Not for me either the Lugentes fields," interrupted Claire, the quiet one who was a teacher, "even though I spent two years on those fields obsessing over a woman who'll never know how much I ached for her."

"Marisol? Are we back to Marisol? Why am I not surprised? Claire, get over it, please, you've been belly-aching for years."

That was Margot again.

But Claire didn't seem to hear Margot.

"We always know when someone loves us, even when we don't want their love. Marisol knows," said Claire. "I know she knows."

"And what about you, Raúl? Have you crossed the *Lugentes campi*?" Claire asked.

Raúl did not answer right away. But then: "Yes, I have. We never recover. Whoever bruised us left a mark that stays there forever. Do we ever recover from our parents? Or from the cruelty of our first arithmetic teacher? Or from someone loved in adolescence? You may seek to recover, and many of us are persuaded we have, until we realize that if we commit the same mistakes time and time again, it's not because we keep choosing the wrong partner or because we don't know how to love, but because new loves won't help us heal from that one ancient wound. All new love can do is mask the wound—and for some, this is good enough."

"Did someone hurt you that much?" asked Margot.

"Yes, once. But only once."

"And?"

"I never discuss it."

"Which tells us you've never recovered," said Margot, clearly pleased to score a point at the expense of the gentleman from Peru.

"It was fate that hurt me, not her. But back to Avernus," he said, clearly trying to change the subject. "If you visit the site of the entrance to the underworld, you'll see where dead souls shamble about complaining of this and that, some with remorse in their hearts, others with regrets, each waiting to be called up to have a say on who they'll want to be once they're brought back to life, not realizing why most keep making the wrong choice each time they're alive again. We come back to correct our lives, because most lives are lived imperfectly."

"Why do they keep making the wrong choice?"

"Why? Because no one wants to accept who they truly are. Everyone requests the self they believe is the very best, hoping to be loved for who they're not and could never be. And the tiny miracle of life, the tiniest yet most imponderable miracle, is when we stumble on people who see us for who we are and want us just for who we are—and these are the ones we spurn the most, the ones we let into our lives with resentment, scorn, and boundless apathy, sometimes even with hatred. But the moment two individuals love each other for who each truly is, then time for them stops, and if these two don't die together, then the partner who lives on never recovers, never forgets, and keeps waiting until they meet again in who knows how many lifetimes. In Shakespeare's own words, *either is the other's mine.* The beloved always comes back. Always will. But the wait is excruciating— they wait not just to live together but also to die together. You see, it's life that is provisional, not love." The group sat stupefied by Raúl's words.

"What I'd love to do is invite all of you tomorrow morning to the bubbling sulfur craters of Pozzuoli, near which, we're told, Aeneas went into the underworld and where Ulysses spoke to dead Achilles and then, without warning, suddenly ran into his mother and said, 'Did you die then too, Mother?' and thereupon tried to embrace her three times, and three times clutched just air.

"Haven't we all embraced air when all we wanted was to hold someone dear to us when they were gone from our lives? We too become air, you know. And just think of all the people we'll never know exist but who embrace us each and every night in their fantasy lives. We're air to them no less than we are air to those we love in secret."

"You make the underworld sound so very real. Is there really such a place?" asked Paul.

"It's in Homer."

"And he never ever lies," said Margot. "You're pulling my leg. I can tell."

Meanwhile, the waiter came to deliver another round of drinks, and a sudden whiff of something rose from their martinis and filled the tiny room.

"What's that incredible smell?" Basil asked.

"It's just the lemons that grow on the Amalfi Coast," said Raúl. "Nothing like them in the world. You don't know what lemon really is until you taste these."

"Here," said Raúl, calling the waiter back and asking him to bring a fresh lemon with a paring knife.

The waiter did as he was asked, and returned with a shiny lemon plus a small, sharp knife.

Raúl held the lemon in his left hand and began to carve out pieces of the rind, which he distributed to Paul and Angelica, then to Basil, and then to every one of those present, including three tourists who happened to overhear Raúl's effusive paean to lemons.

"Have you ever smelled lemons like this?" he asked.

"No, never," came the choral response.

Margot was the last to be given a piece of the rind, and was almost unwilling to take it from Raúl's hand.

"It won't kill you," he said, realizing she was reluctant to have anything to do with lemons—or with him. Yet he did not seem to mind her ill-concealed hostility. She took one sniff, then dropped the rind into the nearest ashtray.

Everyone kept smelling their little sliver of rind, without letting go.

"Now you know why I need to return to Italy every year," said Raúl.

"To smell the rind of a lemon?" Typical Margot sarcasm.

"You may be right," said Raúl. "Sometimes the best things couldn't be simpler: the scent of lemon, a few bars from a Beethoven quartet, the shiny, broad shoulder of a woman in a bathing suit resting on a beach towel, a sea-scape by Dufy, or just the smile on the face of someone you love."

"Can we add Caol Ila from Scotland to the list?"

"And olives from Greece."

"Or mangoes from India?"

"Foie gras from France."

"And five golden rings!" rang Oscar's voice. Everyone burst out laughing.

Then, from nowhere, one of them asked, "When did you learn how to heal people?"

Raúl smiled, as though already sensing that the question, seemingly harmless, was only the opening volley to more questions.

"I probably learned by getting hurt myself and ap-plying a hand to my hurt knee. Everyone instinctively touches the injured part of our body when we've banged it against something. So, I touched my knee. Five sec-onds after I'd touched it, the pain went away. I thought everyone did so. When I played with children my age, whenever someone hurt themselves in the park or the sandbox, they'd immediately place a hand where they hurt. One day I saw a child touch his hurt knee, but his pain wasn't going away and he was crying. So, I literally gave him a hand. And right away his pain was gone.

"He told his mother. I expected the mother to rush to thank me profusely—instead, she warned me never to touch her son again. '*Niente stregonerie, capisci!*' she said, meaning I was a witch. I was convinced I'd done something terribly wrong. From then on, each time someone was hurt, I'd leave them alone, and would watch them suffer.

"When my mother had a kidney stone and woke up one night in terrible agony, I asked her if she could point to the spot where the pain was. I asked her to place my hand on the spot itself, but I didn't want her to know why I was asking, for fear she too would think me a witch. She took hold of my hand and placed it around where the pain radiated. And right away, within the count of a few seconds, the pain was gone. As was her kidney stone, which was tiny and which she passed a few hours later. I denied I had anything to do with it, but from that day on I knew. My mother never spoke about it. But I'm sure she knew. A few years later, when she had an infection on her foot, she asked if I could do something. And of course I did, with the same result."

"How old were you at the time?"

"Seven. But I've known I had that gift since I was two, maybe even younger."

"Do you even remember things as far back as that? No one remembers being three."

Raúl looked down silently at his martini with the lemon rind floating in it and then stared at the rindless little lemon sitting bared and scarred next to the large bowl of peanuts. Everyone sitting in the bar area could sense that something serious had crossed his mind but that he was reluctant to discuss it.

"I go back," he finally said, looking up, and holding his glass as if for sympathy and support, knowing that everyone's eyes were now riveted on him.

"You go back," said Emma. And after a pause: "What does that mean, *you go back*?"

Once again, Raúl looked down at his glass ruefully and was clearly trying to avoid giving explanations. Breaking a small piece from a breadstick that had come with the drinks, he put it into his mouth, as if it were a cigarette.

"This is making me nervous," said Claire.

"Okay, one last question, and then I promise I'll stop," said Emma.

"Go ahead," he said, again with that guileful smile of someone who'd heard all of it so many, many times before. He picked up his paper napkin, wiped some of the condensation around the rim of his glass, and, satisfied with how the glass now looked, took a sip.

"What did you mean by *going back*?" Emma asked.

Again, he looked around the table. "I don't want to upset anyone or make anyone uncomfortable, nor do I want to sound unnecessarily cryptic. But I'll answer this one question and then, please, can we move on to another subject?"

"Okay."

"The point is we all go back. We spend more time than we know trying to go back. We call it fantasizing, we call it dreaming, we give it all manner of names. But we're all crawling back, each in his or her own way. Very few of us know the way, most never find the door, much less the key to the door. We're just groping in the dark. Some of us may even feel we're not from planet Earth but have come down from elsewhere and are all pretending to be normal earthlings. And yet not one of us is. We might as well come from Mars or, as happens to be my case, from a very distant place, or planet, called Peru, which may no longer even exist for me. Some know their way back and some won't ever know."

"And which kind of earthling are you, then?" asked Margot.

"Sometimes I know the way." Then, seeing no one was reacting: "And sometimes I can lead the way."

"Wait, wait," said Emma, "what does *lead the way* mean?"

Suddenly Raúl looked serious. "It means that I can take you back to places you knew long, long before."

"Before what?" asked Emma, growing very impatient.

"Before you were born. Even I could figure that one out," blurted Margot.

But Raúl had read the situation correctly. After hearing such talk, no one in the room could resist thinking of the questions they wished to ask, which explained the sudden silence as each hovered above him like an undecided bird circling the air before finally landing on its branch.

"Let me put it this way. All of us remember having had another self. Which could be a mirage, or a fleeting sense of someone we were long ago, perhaps elsewhere— call it a hinter-self, who feels less transient than we'd like to believe. But here's the catch," he said, stopping midway as if to collect his thoughts. He took another sip.

"And the catch is?" Margot asked, as if unable to stand the silence and determined to be testy, perhaps to prove once and for all that the gentleman from Peru was fabricating the whole thing.

"This other self of ours may not be a bygone self, but a self living elsewhere even as we're having drinks this very minute in this fabulous hotel."

"You mean as in a parallel universe?"

"Call it what you will. But there may be more selves out there: some still unsprung, like tiny egg cells that haven't been fertilized; some already released; and some waiting for the end. Each one of us is a constellation of selves; some are not even lodged in us, but in other people, which is why sometimes we recognize others right away—because they are us in someone else's body."

Raúl grabbed a few peanuts from the bowl and began to chew them ever so slowly.

"How many at this table have at least once called an old phone number that was no longer yours?"

None of those present said they had, but all gave a startled giggle at the question.

"You didn't come out and say you tried, but you all laughed, which proves my point: you've all called an old phone number. And what do you tell the person who picks up the phone, if someone does pick up? Hello, I am an older you, greetings and salutations? Or it could be the other way around: I am the you you haven't quite become yet.

"Or let me ask a different question, then: how many have passed by an old apartment where you used to live once and then looked upstairs to see if the person you were back then still has his lights on?"

Startled giggles again.

"Exactly! And how many have sought out an old love to test if the old lover we once were was still alive in us, only to be totally surprised when we caught ourselves almost willing to start all over again with someone whose last name we couldn't for the life of us recall?"

No answer.

"We may no longer be the person we once were, but what if this person did not necessarily die but continued his life in the shadowland of our own, so that you could say that our life is filled with shadow-selves who continue to tag along and to beckon us in all directions even as we live our own lives—all these selves clamoring to have their say, their time, their life, if only we listened and gave in to them!

"What if we switch roles from time to time, and become the shadow-self of the person we were two minutes ago? And then sideline that new self moments later for a third or a fourth? What if we are no more than a perpetual three-card monte of reshuffled hinter-selves? We traffic in shadow-selves. The old self, the new self, the shadow-self, self number seven or number eleven, the self we always knew we were but never became, the self we left behind and never recovered, the might-have-been self that couldn't be but might still be, though we both fear and hope it might come along one day and rescue us from the person we've had to be all our years.

"But as I said, it's not just the past that haunts us. What haunts us with equal magnitude is what has not happened yet, for there are shadow-selves and shadow-lives waiting in the wings all the time. We are constantly reworking and reinventing both the past and the future. Sometimes we're in the street or in a crowded bus, and we just know: that this person whose glance we caught or whose path we just crossed is another version of someone we know we've loved before and have yet to love again. But that person could just as easily be us in another body. And the beauty of it is that they feel it just as much as we do. Is this other person us or is it someone destined for us whom we keep missing each lifetime? Us in others, isn't this the definition of love?"

Oscar was about to ask a question but then changed his mind and remained silent.

"So, let me close with this thought, since I have your attention but may have bored all of you to death already. The important thing is not knowing that there is or that there was or that there might be another us somewhere. What matters, my friends, is making contact. *Only connect*. The most difficult thing on earth.

"Do you think it is an accident that your boat needed to stop here or that Mark's shoulder hurt or that we are all here having a truly lovely and unusual evening? Maybe, or maybe not. And on that note let us toast with another round of martinis. On me, this time."

Then, suddenly remembering: "Call Malcolm!"

"Wouldn't you already know what he did?" came Margot's snide remark.

"I do know. But I want everyone else here to hear it from him."

Basil right away picked up his phone and dialed New York. When Malcolm answered, Basil put the phone on speakerphone: "I don't know what made me take the advice of some loser type you guys just met at the beach, but just tell him that if I'd given him ten percent of what I managed to rescue thanks to him, he'd be a millionaire."

Raúl snickered at the words *loser type*. "Tell him he owes me nothing and that I was only happy to help. But if he wishes, he could make a generous donation to a foundation for the deaf. A friend I loved was deaf . . ."

Malcolm overheard Raúl's voice and realized he had been put on speakerphone. "Sorry, old man. And thanks so much. Got to run. Let me know if you have any other tips."

Everyone was pleased to hear that Raúl had scored a victory.

"So, you go back?" asked Margot.

"So, I go back," he replied.

"And can you take people with you?"

"You mean like a travel guide for time-travel tourists?"

"If you put it that way."

"I have."

"Whom would you take, if you had a choice?"

Raúl looked around the group of eight. "I'd select Oscar."

"Why me?"

"You'll see. Oscar needs to recall that he once lived in Antwerp and was named Christoffel Loewen," began Raúl. "Christoffel had a very sick mother who, despite her illness, lived a very long life, and as a result of needing constant tending night and day made it impossible for him to find a wife. Or so he wanted it rumored. He could free himself for only two to three hours every day to pen letters for people who did not know how to write or who loved his handwriting and preferred to dictate them to him, but the rest of the time he read and wrote letters— letters to countless individuals in Europe, Russia, North and South America, always in flawless French, which he had learned at school and mastered perfectly. He had a witty pen and everyone he wrote to always responded: writers, composers, philosophers, leaders, including the Count of Cavour, Louis-Philippe, Empress Eugénie, Ivan Turgenev, Franz Liszt. When, years later, his mother died, he was already an old man whose sole passion by then was writing letters and amassing a huge stamp collection with their original letters and envelopes. The collection is priceless. A distant nephew got wind of the collection and, on inheriting all of Christoffel's property, would have sold it to a reputable dealer except that he died a few days before concluding the sale. No one knows of its existence."

"Where is it?"

"It was left in an attic," said Raúl.

"Is the building still there?"

"You mean, hasn't it burned down yet or been bombed during the war? No, it hasn't."

"Do you know the address, by any chance?" asked Oscar.

Raúl laughed.

"Yes, I do. I will give it to you. All you have to do when you show up at the door is say you are the grandson of Christoffel Loewen's nephew and have come to collect a package that was left for you. The old lady who owns the house and who knew the nephew won't be any trouble. You are, in my view, the rightful owner. With your gift of the gab I'm sure you'll charm her."

Oscar was nonplussed, and didn't know whether to truly believe any of it.

"The important thing, as I said, is making contact. There are, as so many physicists will tell you, occasional openings between one time warp and another that are no wider than a sheet of onionskin. Then the slit shuts and you need to wait generations, centuries, who knows, millennia, for the next opportunity."

"Will the visit be worth the trip?"

"Oh, yes," said Raúl. "It will change your life, and allow you to leave your job, pay off your college loans, and sail off with the young sailor who lent you his hat two nights ago."

"You're terrifying," said Oscar, bursting out laughing.

"I know," smiled the gentleman from Peru, looking quite pleased with himself.

"I know you get this all the time, but would you do me a favor?" asked Angelica.

"What?"

"Tell us about us, about me and Paul?"

"Are you under the impression that yours is just love? Seriously, I've watched how you each look at the other when the other isn't watching, and it's almost as if your life is in his life and his in yours. You've been friends since college and you've gone out with god knows how many others—you even got married to a very wealthy man whom you care for but have never and will never love. The decision on what to do is yours entirely. But if I know one thing from my own life, don't wait and don't give up, not now. Behind your love today there are entire lives of missed encounters and chance meetings. Once, you lived in Baltimore and he in Mexico, and you met on a ship headed to, of all places, Anchorage. You both knew, knew right away. But one was in first class, the other in second, and you got off and he stayed on, and you never met again.

"Years and another lifetime later, he was a clerk in a haberdashery and you walked in with your son trying to buy a present for your husband and once again the two of you knew, and neither dared. Does either of you remember the shop?"

Angelica and Paul stared at each other. "No, we don't," one of them said.

"Of course you don't. And yet—"

"—and yet?"

"The shop was in Helsinki, almost abutting a wharf. Think of it together. I'll say no more."

Raúl went on to tell them about the *Lugentes campi*, where all unfulfilled loves are parked, waiting, waiting, waiting.

"Most of us live our lives waiting for the right alignment. For this is what life is: a waiting room. But feel for the dead, who take what they've waited for to the underworld and continue waiting to come back to earth to be made to live again and wait some more. So, better one hour spent doing things we'll regret having done than a lifetime waiting for heaven to touch our lives."

The wannabe lovers looked at each other like teenagers fumbling with the facts of life, almost asking what they should do next. They remembered meeting the first time during registration in New England—but Helsinki, really? They remembered losing each other in school.

"I drifted away hoping you'd come looking for me, but you never did."

"You drifted because you didn't want me to look for you."

"And you met others."

"You knew they were a sham."

"Not after a while."

"Why didn't you at least try?"

"I did try."

"Not that I saw."

"Did you think of her?" asked Raúl.

"All the time."

"And did you know?" he asked Angelica.

"I did know but I stopped believing. He made such a

secret of it. But there wasn't, and still isn't, a single day when I don't catch myself hoping he thinks of me."

Margot, who had been listening with Oscar, couldn't help but throw in: "Helsinki! What were you doing in Helsinki in your previous life?"

"You're asking me? Ask him."

The third round of drinks finally arrived and found everyone sitting down eager to ask Raúl about their own lives.

"Doesn't the passage of time make you sad, though?" asked Claire of Angelica. "Living for the past ten years with someone who could be the wrong man—doesn't that bother you?"

"Yes. It makes me very sad. But what makes me sadder yet is that I may do nothing, despite Paul's admission, or mine. We may decide to lead the wrong life because we've gotten used to it."

"No, no," said Claire. "Tonight feels almost like a midsummer night's dream. Spaces open up, errors are repaired, destinies untangled, and everything can be redressed."

"Is this what this place is for you?" asked Raúl. "Well, look at this bar. With the boat stopped, all of us have stepped out of time. Our troubles are left behind, and our revels hardly started, something good is bound to occur.

"And with this, ladies and gentlemen, I bid you good night. Otherwise, tomorrow at sunrise we'll all be quite a sight."

## Chapter Three

For the next two days, Raúl totally disappeared.

And then, suddenly, there he was, as though he'd been there all along and the three who were coming barefoot up the uneven, ancient steps leading from the beach to the hotel had simply failed to notice him. Angelica, Margot, and Emma. That morning, he was wearing a large straw hat, a pair of soiled shorts, and a T-shirt that had seen better days, and was on his knees with a trowel in hand helping the gardener weed the edge of the stone-paved walk leading to the patio. When he saw them, he stood up, rubbed his dusty hand against his shorts, but sensing he was unable to rid it of dirt, withdrew it with a self-conscious smile.

"You disappeared," said Margot.

"I had to go across to the island to sign some deeds and ended up spending the night there."

He had a sunny disposition that morning and, while staring at them, smiled many more times than he'd done over lunch the first time they had met.

"But here I was trying to finish this little stretch before lunch," he said, surveying the work he'd done, and clearly not displeased with what he'd accomplished that day. "I find this the best therapy in the world. You almost catch yourself talking to the ground, to these stones, to some of these weeds that I must uproot, and to the worms themselves, whom you don't want to disturb, and frankly the silence is so intense and so magnificent. It's the pleasure people take in fishing, if you like fishing, which I hate. I love the heat when it's not so humid. And where are you people coming from?"

"We've just been swimming. Funny you should ask, though," said Margot.

"Why?"

"I thought you knew everything—or had you forgotten?" The dart hit its mark.

"The weather was so wonderful, we lay on the beach, then swam forever, up to the stationary barge," said Angelica, clearly trying to ease out Margot's little dart.

Raúl adjusted his hat, almost looking for something to say, and, finding nothing, looked at Margot.

"I think I've upset you, Margot."

"You mean Marya," she said with a sly look on her face, as though struggling to contain a smile.

"Now you're being cruel to me. I was just trying to apologize for the other day."

"Accepted," she replied.

Her answer had come so swiftly that Raúl saw it as a perfunctory nod to his apology as well as an attempt to fend off formalities. He asked the three of them if they would join him for lunch at two. Emma said she was going back swimming, while Angelica said she was just about to have a very light snack with Paul.

"Why at two?" asked Margot.

"The dining area clears out a bit, and it gets quieter."

"You mean after the young Americans leave the dining area and everyone else goes to nap?"

"Something like that."

She pondered the invitation a tad longer than is usual. "Accepted."

"Will you allow me to order for the two of us now? I usually order what they catch earlier in the day."

She looked at him and smiled. "I said *accepted*."

"Peace, then?"

"We'll see about that."

"Please say yes."

Her smile was meant to convey a tepid *all right*, but he decided to take it as a categorical yes.

"Now I must get back to my weeding, otherwise the gardener will fire me."

At two on the dot she arrived wearing a white linen blouse, baggy white linen trousers, and a sky-blue linen scarf. Her red sandals displayed slim feet that seemed less tanned than he'd noticed earlier that day when she stood barefoot holding her flip-flops on the stone walk to the hotel.

"Am I late?" she asked, sensing that he must have been seated for quite a while. He looked at her, smiled, and simply shook his head to mean *What could have made you think you were late?*

"I always worry."

"Why, are you always late?"

"No, never, but I do worry all the same. My ex used to be the opposite."

"How do you mean?"

"He used to come ahead of time, which always gave me the impression that I'd kept him waiting." Then, on thinking more: "But why am I telling you this?"

"I don't know, why?"

Then, suddenly, with that same sly, quizzical look on her face she'd worn a few hours earlier, she couldn't resist asking, "But you must have known this about me. Don't you know everything?"

"Oh, I see," he said, as they brought the slices of raw fish he'd ordered a couple of hours earlier. The waiter meanwhile explained what sort of fish it was, when it was caught, and which olive oil the chef had used. The oil was a touch peppery, but nothing to intimidate anyone.

"Would you allow me to apologize once again?" he said, ignoring the waiter, who was about to explain the garnish on the vegetable medley but decided to leave them alone.

"You don't have to."

"But I want to."

"Why?"

"I don't know why."

At this they both laughed.

"Contrary to what you think, I don't know everything. Sometimes things just come to me and I am not always able to hold my tongue. But please tell me why I upset you so much."

"I'm not sure I know either."

"Was it the truth about your name or your birthday that you didn't want to hear, or was it just my excavating private facts about Basil's twin that bothered you?"

"Maybe both. The fact is, it scared me how you could be so totally right about things that no one knew a thing about and that those who did had totally forgotten. It frightened me, especially about the cannibalized twin. Or maybe I didn't want to hear that at all."

"So sorry." He reached out and placed his right palm

over her left hand. She did not remove her hand. But he removed his.

"This will be fantastic fish, I promise," he said, changing the conversation.

"Do you know everything about fish as well?" she asked as she cut a slice. This, he figured, was a tacit little jab. But he liked it.

"Absolutely not. In fact, I know nothing about cooking."

"You never cook for yourself?"

"Almost never."

After the raw fish appetizer came another fish, this time grilled. They had a salad, then dessert, all accompanied by one of the best white wines of the region. At the end of their meal they were served a grappa.

It was nearing four when they decided to order a second round of grappa. After the tall septuagenarian waiter had finished pouring, Raúl finally told her how happy he was that she had accepted his invitation to lunch.

"Moments like these happen so rarely in life. I just hope I'm not keeping you from your friends."

"You're not keeping me from my friends," she said, echoing his very words to suggest a touch of humor. "But then, you knew I was free this afternoon, didn't you?"

"I know facts, or the general contour of facts, not feelings or what goes on in someone's mind. Which is why I've not always been lucky in my life when it comes to people. I'm not sure I've ever learned how to read people."

"You don't look like the sort who misreads people or who's been unlucky in life."

He gave a heedless half shrug, half nod. "I've been

lucky in my life. True. But there again, lucky in facts, lucky with things, but not in what mattered most to me."

She stopped drinking from her tiny grappa glass and held it in midair. "Meaning love?"

"Exactly."

"Has anyone really been lucky when it comes to love?"

"A few have. Not many. But I know some who have," he said with doubt still lining his features, which meant he wasn't entirely convinced, which is why the two of them ended up laughing.

"Aren't you married?" she asked.

"I've been married. Once when I was in my thirties, and once eleven years ago. And there have been people in between, but now that I look back, I realize I've never loved any of the women I've lived with."

"Not one?"

"Well, one, yes."

"Was this recently?"

"No, when I was in my early twenties. The ones before her I don't remember at all, and those who came after were just stopgaps, placeholders, fillers. When I look back . . ." But he didn't finish his sentence.

The silence that hung between them on that mild afternoon was not unpleasant. She threw her head back to better enjoy the weather and the late-afternoon light, or perhaps it was simply her body showing how pleased she was to be spending a quiet afternoon this way. When he looked down, he saw that she had removed her red sandals and was resting her feet on the warm gravel. He could hear her raking the pebbles with her toes, softly, slowly. When they had finished drinking, he asked if she would take a walk with him, not too far from the hotel grounds. She didn't say no. He put on his straw hat and, before stepping onto the dirt road outside the hotel lobby, stood still for a moment. "I love the sound," he said.

"What sound?"

"The total silence. Turtledoves far, far away, the clamor of one or two kids playing in the bay, the occasional lawn mower droning quietly on a pleasant summer afternoon while everyone is still napping. I never nap."

"I never nap either."

"Yes, I know."

She nodded.

"Have I been forgiven?" he asked.

She smiled at him. "The jury is still out."

Then, not wanting to misread her, he said, "I think my sentence has just been commuted. See what a simple but wonderful lunch can accomplish?"

Without replying, she shifted her foot in her sandal.

"Come. We'll take a short walk."

She thought he was going to take her along the shore; instead he led her outside the hotel grounds, then up a hill that was covered with marine pines. It led to a narrow unpaved road that finally worked its way through what looked like a wood. The wood was unusually silent and gave off an air of intense peace and tranquility she had seldom encountered before. She stopped and breathed in the scent of pines. They stood watching the landscape without uttering a word. Neither seemed to mind the silence between them. "Heavenly," she said.

"Isn't it?" he added, and he too stopped to breathe in the light afternoon air. "A few more yards and we're there," he said.

When they reached the end of the wood, they arrived

at a flat plot of land, "the field of melons," he said. The smell there was overpowering and enticingly sweet and stirred a bewildering sense of hunger, which the act of eating could never soothe, the way, he said, certain scented soaps stimulate a desire to bite into them, which everyone knows not to do.

Finally, they arrived at a garden that boasted exotic plants that had never been planted elsewhere in Europe. "The son of the original owner of more than a century ago," he explained, "had sailed to the Far East and brought back seeds, which he secretly planted against his father's wishes. This is why the garden was hidden in the woods. He spent years planting these fruit trees in secret until his father's death. But by then the garden had blossomed and could no longer be moved. So, it stayed hidden here. Many of the plants perished, of course, but some survived and thrived." Was she interested in plants and gardens? he asked.

"Not at all," she replied. "Or didn't you know?"

"I suspected," he replied, smiling to signal he was aware of her insinuation. "Still, I wanted to show you something."

After pushing a gate that grated loudly against the ground before letting them inside, he turned around to let her take in a view of the other bay that she had never known existed. Under the spellbinding afternoon sun, it felt as though they were standing a mile above the sea.

"Is this what you wanted to show me?"

"No," he replied. "This here is the spice garden—of no interest to people who are not interested in gardening," he added after bending down and rubbing his hand on a plant that stood knee-high. He then brought his palm to her nose: "Smell this."

"What is it?" she said, brusquely withdrawing her face from the reach of his palm.

"Smell it first."

"Yes, but what is it?" she kept asking before consenting to smell it.

"You don't trust me, do you? Here, rub your hands on these leaves and smell." She finally relented. She seemed surprised.

"I know this smell. Reminds me of something, but I can't tell what."

"It's lovely, isn't it?" Then, giving her time to reflect, he added: "Almost like lemongrass, but not lemongrass, and like lavender, but not lavender. And yet I'll bet you've never smelled it before, though it stirs something like memory, but then not memory. Shakes up your limbic system, though, doesn't it?"

"But I know it." She leaned down and tore a stem off the plant to take with her. "I love this scent," she said.

As they continued to walk over the muddy ground, they eventually came upon a small hut where a gardener sat on a stool, repairing a rake.

"*Commendatore*," he said, rising to his feet.

Raúl greeted him and told him that he wanted to borrow the long pole to shake some fruit from the tree for the signorina.

"Does everyone know you here?" she asked.

"I spent all my summers here. None of those who grew up in this area have moved, and all have kept the same jobs. Time stops here. In fact, when I come here, I do nothing. I like doing nothing. You saw me working the hotel grounds. That's the most I do."

The gardener went into the shed and came out with an old pole.

He offered it to Raúl but then said he would be perfectly willing to knock some of the fruit off for him. But Raúl said he'd do it himself, he'd been doing it since childhood.

"I wanted you to tell me what you thought. It's not a passion fruit, but it has a nuance of passion fruit and of pomegranate, maybe guava. But no one knew what to call it, so they called it *frutta dell'ira*, fruit of wrath, though no one knows why, possibly because the owner of the land hated that his son was planting so many exotic plants and trees here and kept scolding him. Or maybe because the fruit has growths like goose bumps and overgrown pimples and turns so red at this time of the year."

As they approached the tree, she thought she saw something move. "There are all manner of birds here, but they're very timid, and quiet. Follow me." When they finally reached a tall, lean tree, he pointed to what looked like full-blooded ruby spiky pears at the topmost reaches of the tree. "Hence the pole," he said. "I used to rob this tree of so much fruit once." And having said that, he started poking one of the fruits until it was finally freed from its twig and came tumbling down through stems and branches. He managed to catch it with both his hands.

He inserted both thumbs into it, opened it, and released a huge number of very tiny black seeds that looked like caviar or guava seeds. "Sometimes they have tiny worms inside, but this one is totally clean. Want to try a taste?"

"*Frutta dell'ira?*" She questioned its name.

"*Frutta dell'ira.* My mother used to peel off the skin, remove all the seeds, then slice up the fruit and let the whole thing sit in lemon juice. It was naturally quite sweet, which is why she added salt. I have the most amazing memories of this fruit salad. But ever since she died, no one makes this dessert any longer."

"Did you grow up here?"

"Only during summers. Our house is on the other side of the hill. I'll take you there sometime."

"When?" The suddenness of her question surprised him. He looked at her and smiled.

"Tomorrow, if you like."

"Are we having lunch too?"

"If you wish, of course."

"Will you order the exact same thing?"

"Yes, easily. But don't you find me boring?"

"No."

"Maybe slightly?"

"Well, yes, especially when you ask like this." She tasted the fruit, pondered, finished her half of it while he bit into his half, all the while watching her.

"Pomegranate but not pomegranate. Maybe guava, but not guava."

He looked at her, baffled. It took him a moment to realize she was teasing by using words he'd spoken moments earlier.

"Ever had this before? Bring back any memories?"

"Very, very vaguely. But I don't know of what. But it is sweet."

He did not wait to be asked and, using the rod, released another fruit. But he did not let go of the rod in time, so the fruit came crashing down, splattering its contents on the ground.

"Pity."

He tried for another. This time she caught it. She did

what he had done and pressed it open, and breaking a twig from one of the trees, she used it to scrape off the seeds.

She liked the fruit. "The fruit salad shouldn't be too difficult to make. I wonder why they call it *frutta dell'ira*."

"And I thought you weren't interested in plants or gardens."

She told him she was a good cook.

"Yes, I know," he said, then caught himself. "Let's go back," he added.

"So, lunch tomorrow, then?" she asked.

"Same time, same spot," he replied.

They returned the way they had come and parted at the entrance to the hotel, where her friends were waiting for a swim.

"Tomorrow, come with a bathing suit. I'll show you the Baia di Montesacro, a place no one knows exists."

She waved goodbye, and had already taken off her sandals. "And thank you for lunch."

He shrugged his shoulders to mean no need for thanks, no fussy formalities, no pressure, it was, after all, entirely his pleasure.

## Chapter Four

When he arrived, she was already seated at his table. He removed his sunglasses and was happy to notice that she had taken his seat, most likely to allow him to have the shade this time.

She was wearing a straw hat, the top of her bathing suit, and a skirt. "I did what you said."

He was wearing shorts, a loose linen shirt, a cotton sweater with the sleeves wrapped around his neck, and, like her, a straw hat. "Still, a lovely surprise," he said.

"I thought this was the plan."

"Yes, I know, but I'm still very happy we're having lunch again."

By then almost all the tables had been set for dinner and the patrons had left. "I've ordered the exact same things I ordered yesterday." The same white wine, the same raw fish salad, and as for the fish, it was indeed the same as the previous day's, except it was that day's catch.

"But we'll try a different dessert," he said.

"No *frutta dell'ira* ice cream?"

"If only!"

He liked that she remembered, liked that she didn't hide recalling its name.

"Enjoy the wine, because on a day like today, it is the most amazing thing on planet Earth."

"I agree."

"After we're done, I'll show you a couple of spots tourists never see."

The appetizers came. She ate her roll, then borrowed some of his, then simply took all of it. He enjoyed watching her eat. She noticed he was looking at her. Finally, she said, "You're staring."

"Yes, I am."

She gave a faint, quiet smile, then continued cutting her fish. "Why?"

"Because I like that we are friends."

She gave a pensive nod. "Me too."

"Most people won't say this," he said.

"But I do."

When they were done, and standing up, he watched her slip her feet easily back into the red sandals he had admired less than twenty-four hours earlier.

They walked along the *strada bianca*. Except for the few salespeople headed hastily to their gift shops, the road was totally empty under the intense afternoon sun. Margot had to stop a moment, complaining that a pebble had gotten into her sandal and was bothering her. She leaned on his shoulder as she removed her sandal, couldn't find the pebble, then shook the sandal some more before putting it back on. He noticed that her sandal had left a slim x-shaped pattern of lighter skin on her otherwise tanned foot.

"Is it far?" she asked.

"Not at all."

Within ten minutes they had reached the end of a road that led to the highway. "Almost there," he said. And sure enough, they stepped over an old, collapsed, weather-beaten wooden fence that opened the way to the shore, and then they proceeded down the very slim arm of land that cut deep through the bay and then curved inward, almost creating a semicircle, which explained why not even a ripple reached the shore here. There was no sign of civilization, as though neither the Greeks nor the Romans nor the original inhabitants of the area had ever touched this spot of land where even the aged olive trees, which grow in phalanx formation elsewhere on the Italian peninsula, were scattered wildly about and seemed untended by human hands. As elsewhere in the area, the tireless chorus of cicadas and the moan of turtle-doves. It was the most peaceful spot on earth, and the sea, under the languorous midafternoon light, was as calm and limpid as a beautiful pair of sloe eyes that never shed tears.

"Does anyone swim here?"

"People did once. But everyone prefers the crowded resort beaches. Want to try?"

She nodded.

"I still come here in the morning. No one, not a single soul, ever comes. And when you want shade, the ancient olive groves are happy to oblige. There are fig trees behind, and the figs are free for the taking come August through September."

She wanted to walk along the shore and dip her toes in the water.

"This is my spot," he said, and began removing his clothes down to his swimsuit.

She hesitated for an instant, but he had turned his

back and let her undress. She even removed her watch and her necklace and simply dumped them on her clothes. She still looked around nervously, as though uncertain there really was no one, then raced toward the water.

By that hour of the day the sunlight had grown diffuse and the glare more muted, and once the two had swum out till their feet could no longer touch bottom, they treaded water, feeling a sense of plenitude and pure bliss wash over them. "Look behind you," he said, pointing to the shore. When she turned to look, the bay suddenly appeared so very distant and more deserted and more paradisiacal than she could have imagined.

"There's not a thing to want here," he said.

"You're so right."

"This, according to legend, is possibly where the lotus-eaters lived."

"You mean Ulysses's companions who refused to sail back to Ithaca? I can see why now," she said, once again making light of her college education.

"I love walking all the way here, love reading here under the shade of one of those trees, and then love the walk back, with sand still in my sandals, which takes me back to my childhood, when I used to hate having sand trapped in my sandals and preferred walking barefoot. Coming here reminds me that I do love planet Earth, that I like being alive, that I might even like myself."

"Don't you always feel like this?"

"No," he replied, almost too rapidly. "I already told you. No one I know does. Some pretend to, others try hard to fool themselves, but no one likes who they truly are, except in spurts. When I feel the sun on my skin and the water nearby and happen to like where I am, I try my best to coddle the feeling. The only other things that come close for me are chamber music and tennis."

"And nothing else?"

"Sometimes that too. But not always." They decided to go farther out. "You swim well!" he said.

"Parents. Came with tennis and piano lessons. You're a good swimmer yourself."

"This was my beach once upon a time. I used to come here with my mother, then I got in the habit of coming alone, and then with someone special."

"The one and only?"

"The one and only."

"What would you pay me not to tell my friends about this stretch of beach?"

"You won't tell them."

"How do you know?" she asked, dunking underwater, then coming back up and throwing her hair back while passing both palms along her face and nose.

"Because this is our spot, yours now and mine, and no one else's," he replied, then looked away at the distant eastern arm of the bay.

"Proprietary, aren't we!" she said.

"Maybe. Yes."

He asked if she could spot the very tip of the land extension before them. She said she could. He told her that there used to be a structure there once and asked if she had any idea what it might have been. They'd taken it down decades before.

She thought for a moment, then said, "I suppose a lighthouse. Most likely abandoned at least a century and a half ago."

"Why abandoned?"

"Just a hunch. What would a lighthouse be doing here, anyway?"

He agreed with her. They both said it would have been a small lighthouse. "Striped black and white, you think?" he hazarded.

She thought awhile. "No. I suspect it must have been more like a squat little hut made of stacked boulders with a strange round attic-looking structure from which scant light emanated to warn mariners of rocks and shoals. But I doubt it even gyrated as lighthouses do elsewhere."

"When I was a boy," he said, "there used to be such a structure there, but totally abandoned in those days. My mother once told me that it was used by the Germans during the war. I was never allowed to go near there for fear of unexploded mines underfoot. But eventually, once you swam to the rock where we're headed, you could actually walk along the very shallow edge of land and reach the lighthouse."

They continued to swim till they reached the large rock. "As an adolescent I used to come here to be alone. Like being on another planet and stepping totally out of time. A wonderful feeling of pure quiet and pure being at one with the world."

"I've never felt such wonderful water before," she said. "I even like its taste."

"Welcome to the Tyrrhenian Sea."

He climbed on the rock and sat on what was clearly his usual spot. Then he reached with his hands for hers and helped her climb up.

"Do you always bring women up here?"

"Never."

"Except for the one and only?"

"The one and only, yes. But that's forty years and two months ago."

"And how many days?"

"I can tell you if you need to know." She did not answer.

"We used to bring fruit and sit as we're doing now."

"Dark grapes, I'm betting?"

"Yes, there's something about seawater and fruit. Then I realized what it was. Salt makes fruit sweeter."

"Next time we'll remember to bring fruit. How about the *frutta dell'ira*?"

"That was her favorite. We spent hours sitting on this rock, just as we're doing now. And we spoke, spoke so much, and laughed even more than we spoke." He stopped for a second. "I'm happy you're here, though."

"Though?" she immediately asked.

"I meant, I'm happy it's you here."

She didn't know exactly what to add, or whether she'd understood his answer. She paused. "I find myself . . . I find myself strangely envious of her, of the two of you, and I don't even know why."

"We were so young at the time, so young. Nothing held us back." He found himself deflecting the subject, as though something hovered between them and neither wished to bring it up.

"From here we can swim to the very tip of the eastern arm of the bay."

She nodded.

"Afterward we'll either walk to where we left our clothes, or swim back. Then we'll dry on the sand. With this heat one dries in no time."

They visited the spot where the lighthouse once stood and where the Germans had set up a makeshift post, then swam back to shore. They waited a short while, then walked to the fallen fence and there, having dried themselves, put on their clothes.

He gave her his cotton sweater, which she slipped on over her head, tugging down the sleeves. She liked its smell. It surprised her. "This was just lovely," she said. "I wonder what people will think seeing me arrive wearing your sweater."

"They can think whatever they please."

Without putting their sandals on but letting their feet drag through the sand to dry faster, they reached the end of the eastern arm of land, which suddenly looked more like a jetty extending far off into the water and into sunlight.

As they continued walking he bent down and picked up a pumice stone, then offered it to her.

"I haven't seen a real wild pumice stone in my life. Thank you. Those they sell nowadays in the States have such tiny holes, they look and feel like pieces of cement cut small to fit your palm."

She toyed with the stone and seemed fascinated by its lightness. "Should we head back?" she asked.

"Soon. I'll take you by way of a shortcut. It's on the other side of the hill. Much prettier."

The shortcut Raúl had in mind lay hidden off the coast and crossed the main street of the adjacent town. And indeed, as they approached, Margot saw that it was milling with tourists and vacationers stopping at one high-end shop after another, with the occasional gelato vendor, enoteca, or espresso bar.

"Unbelievable, but this used to be a dirt-poor fishing hamlet once—now it's a beautified Potemkin village. Its stores used to sell fruits, vegetables, and always fish."

Raúl stepped inside one of the bars, purchased two small bottles of sparkling water, and handed Margot a bottle.

"How did you know I was dying for water?"

"Why didn't you say anything?"

"Actually, I didn't think of it."

They stopped for a short while as they drank.

"This is exactly like every tourist town on both Italian coastlines. One boutique after the other, with the de rigueur porcelain shop bearing regional patterns and motifs that are manufactured and painted elsewhere."

"Were none of these stores here?"

"Not one."

"What was this, a bus depot?"

"And what else?"

She looked around her and couldn't begin to know what this town had once been.

"Just take a guess," he prodded.

"A garage? A movie theater?" And then she corrected herself. "A slaughterhouse?"

"What made you guess a slaughterhouse?" he asked.

"No idea." She looked around and saw a plaque that read *Piazza del Macello*. "Maybe because I read the plaque without realizing it."

"Do you even know what *macello* means in Italian?"

"No."

"Then how could it have helped you guess what used to be here?"

"I don't know. Why are you cross-examining me?"

"Am I upsetting you?"

"A little, yes."

"Why?"

"I don't know why, but you are."

He explained that he simply wanted to show her how this rinky-dink little place had become, from nothing, a hotbed of high-end shops. "Take a look at this triple cinema, playing the same superhero film in all three theaters. In my day there was no cinema here."

"What was there?" She looked at the theaters, trying to visualize what he was remembering.

"Any child could tell you that."

"What, a bus depot for some of those tiny buses running up and down the coast?"

"And near the depot?"

"How would I know. A winery? You're quizzing me again."

"No, I'm not."

"Yes, you are."

"Okay, so I was a bit. This whole new building, which is made to look Gothic, was something else in my day. It was a huge, helter-skelter, improvised amusement park that lasted only a few weeks each summer. My parents used to take me there. Then, the poles and tents and swing carousels and bumper cars would suddenly disappear until the following year."

They walked up a narrow road neatly paved with cobblestones that were embedded into the ground in arched patterns. When they reached the top of the hill, they found a lovely tea hut with crowded tables and chairs where those who had come for shopping were taking a rest. Beyond the teahouse they spotted a large rectangular nineteenth-century villa surrounded by rich vegetation and a flower garden, next to which stood a similar house, but much smaller, built to seem like its younger sister. Both houses had mansard roofs and looked nothing like any building in southern Italy.

"Feels like Normandy," she said.

"Not surprising. The man who had it built was a Frenchman who wanted a French home overlooking the Tyrrhenian Sea. By the way, it leads directly down the hill to the beach where we swam. Come, I'll take you there."

"You've been there before?"

"More times than I remember. This used to be our summer home. The smaller house was a guesthouse and a haven when we were kids, since this was where all the children of my parents' friends stayed."

They walked up the hill and rang the bell. There was the sound of children playing inside.

Eventually they heard steps and a lady opened the door. She immediately exclaimed Raúl's name and hugged him affectionately. They bandied their usual jokes: *You never come! You know I can't stand you. But we love you. Plus, your food is horrible.* Turning to Margot, Raúl informed her that Doriana was a Cordon Bleu chef. Introductions were made, Doriana insisted on serving tea. Margot said it wasn't necessary. Doriana persisted, Margot relented.

"You're worse than he is," Doriana said, as Margot and Raúl entered the house. "And I thought no one could be worse."

"I wanted to show her the house. We'll stay for your horrible tea and cookies."

And with that Doriana hopped into the kitchen, screaming at the children who massed around her when they heard the English word *cookie.*

"Next autumn they're all going back to boarding school," said Doriana, "and I'll be done with the lot of them and finally have time to finish my book on the terrible end of Masaniello." Then, turning to Margot: "I'm just a historian."

"Come, I'll show you around," said Raúl.

He walked her through the hallway, then into the dining room, which led to a large terrace from which, once he opened the large French windows, one could watch the sea. It was a spellbinding, expansive view of the very-late-afternoon blue. Raúl and Margot caught a view of the shore as well as the rock where they had lounged for a while, with a clear sight of the strip of land extending out into the sea like a ballerina's gesture of worship and insouciance.

He closed the windows and walked her to the living room.

"I could have sworn there was a piano here," she said.

"Here?" he asked.

"No, over there."

"I don't know. Could have been. Maybe they moved it."

"Yes, because where else would they have put the dark baroque bench with the carved lion head on each armrest?"

"What armrests with what lions' heads? I should know, I grew up in this house."

"I was just imagining it," she said.

He took her to the library. The books hadn't moved in more than a century. "See that love seat over there?" He pointed at it. "I used to read there. My little universe: Stendhal, Forster, Hardy, and my favorites, Thucydides, Herodotus, and Xenophon."

"A love seat all to yourself!"

"This room was my kingdom. It hasn't changed one bit. Not the love seat, not the vases and ugly marble statuettes, not the memories always cluttering in. Let me take you upstairs."

On the stairway up, however, she suddenly stood still, turned around, and, looking out of the bay windows in the library, simply said: "I know I've been here before."

He did not say anything, but stared at the afternoon glow upon the stairs and to himself muttered, "I know."

## Chapter Five

Doriana called them downstairs for tea on the veranda.

"This is such a beautiful house," said Margot.

Doriana looked at her and smiled. "It took forever for him to decide to let us live in it," she said, pointing at Raúl. "We changed so very little, except for the children's rooms. Even the china hasn't changed, cracked and chipped as everything is in this house. But then we like it that way.

"Look at this dish," she added. "Pure Limoges, but defaced thanks to the dishwasher, which we were told would scrape all the colors away and blandify everything. But did we listen?"

"The way you cook would scrape off the lining of every human stomach," Raúl said.

"He never comes, no matter how many times I invite him."

"And with good reason," he retorted.

Margot took her cup and held it in both hands, then removed her red sandals and tucked both her feet on the bar under Raúl's wicker chair. "This is heaven," she finally said.

"You are welcome to come here anytime—not him, though!"

"Don't trust her. She'll cook dinner for you and the next thing is you won't tolerate anyone else's cooking, including your own. She's a Circe in the kitchen. After her chicken Marengo, you'll never be able to eat anyone else's chicken. To say nothing of her tarte Tatin! Ruins you for life."

A moment of silence followed as all three sipped their tea and watched the setting sun cast glowing colors on the horizon.

"It's so peaceful here," said Margot. "The strange thing is that this is all too familiar, as if I've been on this very patio before."

"Well, the house was designed by a French architect who built so many houses on the same model that it wouldn't surprise me if you've been in others as well. You'll find his houses in Poland and Hungary."

"No, I've been here, in this house, on this very patio."

Margot swore that there was a piano downstairs and a wooden love seat with sunken cushions and two armrests bearing the carved features of two lions' heads. "Plus, I'm almost sure I've been in the library, and especially up and down the stairway in the afternoon. And yet, I know this is my very first time here. I've never even been to the south of Italy before."

"A déjà vu!" exclaimed Doriana, chewing on a biscuit.

Margot smiled back, but suddenly stiffened. She removed her feet from under Raúl's chair, put down her cup on the wrought-iron table with pointed metal leaves, looked around her, and, turning to Raúl, said: "If I believed in spells, I'd say I was under one. Am I under a spell?"

"Do people still believe in spells?" asked Doriana. "You remind me of my grandmother."

"Then what is happening? I can even recognize the patterns on the china now, faded or not," said Margot.

"But everyone owns this kind of china the world over, you'll find it in any shop."

Margot picked up her teacup again, but then put it back down on the table.

"I know where the bathroom is. And I know this house. I even know where an old sewing machine used to be." And turning to Raúl, said: "Explain." And seeing he hesitated: "Now!"

This was the moment he had feared the most. Leading up to it had been fun, even sweet, but this now was pure agony.

"Let's start with the lighthouse," he said, "then move on to the bus depot, then the slaughterhouse, finally the amusement park. We'll even throw in *frutta dell'ira*."

"Yes, and?"

"You were amazingly right each and every single time. You were even right about the rock when we sat on it."

"What did I say?"

"You spoke about grapes."

"What about the grapes?" There were signs of vexation on her face.

"Would you let me explain?"

"Yes, go ahead, explain. Right now!"

"Just let me proceed at my own pace," he said, giving her a chilling, momentary glance.

He stood up, went to a bookcase, and took down a large picture book of old black-and-white photographs taken by Luigi Alberti. "Every family in the area owns this book," he said, "because it captures the landscape as it was immediately after the war." He opened the book to the little town they had just visited. Here was the bus depot, there the amusement park, there the slaughter-house, and just in case she had any doubts, on the cover of the book was a faded sepia picture of the long arm of the bay with a tiny square shed at its very tip—"Just as you described it," he said, "the lighthouse.

"But let me give you some background." And so, he began to tell her about a young man whose family summered every year in southern Italy. The young man's uncle, who lived in England, had a twenty-two-year-old daughter. He and his wife were involved in such bitter divorce proceedings that they asked if the family might house their daughter in Italy for a few months before she was to return to Oxford later that autumn. She couldn't have been happier than to be spared the daily riot in her parents' home, where quarrels, insults, and objects thrown around the dining room made her life intolerable.

But the student, as everyone would find out within a few days after she'd settled in their home late that spring, was hardly more tolerable than her parents. She was uncommonly impatient and harsh with the help in the house, and her speech and behavior were downright offensive with everyone, including her uncle, her mother's brother, who took her blunt manner in his stride and put up with her insolence whenever she criticized or mocked their home. She had taken up the bad habit of practicing her violin in their living room for hours on end, which made family life impossible past midmorning. Her morning snack was always left half-finished in the living room, and her coffee mug left round stains on one of the wooden cabinets.

But worst of all was her attitude toward the young man in the household. She contradicted and argued with everything he said and made no effort to hide her contempt for him. One evening, just a few days after she had moved in, she watched him walk into the living room to bid his parents good night. He was on his way to a dinner party and was wearing a new suit. She looked him over, smirked, and said it was clear the suit was purchased off a rack somewhere. His tie didn't go with his shirt, the shirt was too bright, the sleeves too long, and the jacket too wide. Had he, perhaps, purchased it expecting to put on weight in the years to come?

He was humiliated.

"These are no better," she said after he'd rushed upstairs and taken off the suit, shirt, and tie she'd derided and put on other clothes.

He began to dislike her even more. What particularly galled him was the way she was so visibly enamored of herself. Every time she passed by a mirror or a dark glass panel, she could not resist casting a lingering look at herself, always checking her shirt, her hair, her face. Sometimes, when she spoke with someone, it was clear her eyes were focusing not on the person to whom she was speaking, but on her face in the mirror.

For her part, she couldn't stand his snobbish air each time he attempted to play master of the house when his father wasn't present. It was clear to everyone that once he'd passed his law exams, he'd manage his father's affairs and eventually inherit his business. It was also very clear that he resented her presence and wanted her and her violin gone long before she was due back to either one of her beleaguered parents.

That summer he was cramming for the bar, and the

last thing he needed was an intruder upsetting his quiet home rituals with the perpetual droning of her instrument in their living room. Worse yet was her horrible habit of humming with her violin, sometimes literally singing along with the instrument. His mother tried a few times to speak to her about the sound and recommended she practice in another room, far from where her son was studying.

So here he was studying for the bar and there she was singing along, almost as though doing it on purpose. Finally, one day, he decided to take matters into his own hands and asked her to stop practicing while he was studying. She asked if he would stop studying while she practiced. Well, he had an exam, he said. And so did she, she replied. Then she should practice in her own home, not in his. They had a loud row at which he blew up and told her that she was not his sister and that this was not her home. "Besides, you're not even your parents' daughter," he added with a heavy note of sarcasm.

"Meaning what?" she said with derision tearing out of her voice.

"Meaning exactly what I've just said."

She seemed puzzled.

"So, you don't know, do you?" he finally asked.

"Don't know what?"

He was not the type to mince words and told her that she and her parents didn't have a speck of blood in common; that her parents, who were second cousins, had more in common with each other than with her.

"You, dear girl," he said, "were adopted. No one knows who brought you into this world, so you are what is generally referred to as a mongrel."

This shut her up. She was certain that he had made

the whole thing up to hurt her, but as happens with unexpected revelations that suddenly seem to put everything in its place, his words had come with the ring of truth and, surprisingly, didn't upset her—as though she had always suspected but hadn't had the time or the means or the will to consider the matter further. But what surprised her even more than the revelation itself was the feeling of total relief that accompanied what she'd just heard, as if she had finally found a good reason to be rid of parents she'd wished to shun since childhood.

She had always had a strange hunch that she never belonged to them, but where that hunch was born, she had no idea. Still, this did not mean that she was going to accept the news from him. She yelled the loudest "Liar!" anyone had ever screamed in his placid household and, after slapping him in the face, asked him to give her one iota of proof.

"You don't need proof. Your rage is proof enough," he replied. No woman had ever slapped him before. It spoke of her sudden helplessness, and he liked having driven her to it. Seeing him smile after the slap sent her spiraling into a fit, and she was about to scratch him on the face except that he grabbed both her wrists and asked if it wasn't time for her to start practicing her fiddle now.

"You monster, you shithead." Then she got ahold of herself. "This news, for your information, is nothing new. The only difference now is that you're the shithead who's dotted the i's for me. Now leave the room."

"No, you leave."

She walked straightaway out of the living room, muttering, "You beast!" This is what she'd heard her mother exclaim to her father, neither of whom, as she'd just found out, was her parent. "And good riddance to the whole lot of you," she yelped. She slammed the door shut behind her.

But later that day, thinking back on what he had told her, he realized he had gone too far. He knew now that she had every reason to hate him. He could already tell she hated everything about him, from the way she grimaced when he read verses out loud to his mother or the way she sighed each time he rubbed his hands with sunblock, just his hands, before heading out to the beach. He could see it in her eyes, or when she grunted when he thought he was saying something profound while watching the news. He was stuffy and fussy, and he seemed to know it and liked being that way, which is why she had cut him down on the evening he put on a suit before heading out to dinner with friends. She hated the way he rattled the car keys, hated the sound of his shoes when they hit the parquet floor, hated his laugh even. She even hated his horrible habit of pruning the membrane off every mandarin segment, off every orange, or grapefruit, because he didn't like the skin of citrus fruit, and would leave their naked sloughs drying on his plate like the shed skin of baby reptiles. He even wanted his tomatoes peeled, ditto with potatoes and cucumbers. There was not a thing she liked about him. Now she wanted him dead. And he could read it on her features. It amused him, as if he wanted her to hate him, because he enjoyed hating her.

When his father asked him to apologize to her for something he had said, he refused, saying he'd never apologize to someone like her. He said this because he had heard his father ask her to apologize to him for something she had said that might have hurt his feelings.

Her blunt reply was unforgettable: *I don't know how to apologize.*

Yet, despite their recent rows—and there were many— both were discreet enough not to let on to his parents how much they scorned each other or that he had told her the truth about her adoptive parents. At dinner the two of them were well behaved: "Could you pass me the salt?" "Of course. Here it is." This the day after she had called him a beast. At breakfast, when they were seldom alone, they greeted each other with a seemingly hearty "Good morning," and when watching TV with the family on the evenings when neither was out, they always shared the same sofa. When they crossed each other either on the way in or out of the house or in the empty corridor, he would whisper "Asshole," and she would whisper back "Shithead." Once, on the stairs, and without meaning to, he accidentally elbowed her rather hard, while she right away kicked his shin with the edge of her sneaker. He yelled in pain. "Teaches you," she said. Then, when she happened to trip against a breeze block in the garden, he couldn't help exclaiming, "Hope it hurts."

But when he saw her bleeding from her wrist after she had cut herself against the large, pointed, slightly protruding leaf of a wrought-iron table in the garden, he rushed to fetch a spool of gauze from one of the medicine cabinets and applied rubbing alcohol generously on the cut before wrapping the gauze tightly three times around her wrist. He couldn't decide which had given him more pleasure as he helped stanch the bleeding: proving useful in a moment of need and showing his expertise in treating a wound, or watching her reaction when the alcohol burned her. "You did it on purpose," she said, referring to the alcohol. He smiled, all the while applying pressure to the cut with his thumb as he tied the knot around it.

"I did," he said.

"There's no need for so much alcohol."

"At least you won't need stitches."

"I'm not an idiot," she cried, meaning any idiot could tell that stitches weren't needed.

"Well, you are an idiot," he said, and left her in the garden with the bottle of alcohol and roll of gauze for her to return to the medicine cabinet.

"Right," she replied. "Don't let me hold you up."

But he was already gone and out of earshot.

Later that same afternoon when she was lying on the beach, he passed by with a glass bottle of cold water. "Can I have a sip of water?" he heard her say. "I forgot to bring my own." Without thinking he threw the bottle on the sand next to her. She was not unaware of his contemptuous gesture, but was thirsty enough not to show any sign of anger or say anything about his manner. She simply brushed the sand off the bottle, removed the cap, and took a few sips. Seeing that some sand had landed on her towel as well, she brushed it away, then, raising her eyes, looked at him and made a gesture to give him back his bottle. "Why do you hate me?" she suddenly asked.

He did not have time to think of an answer and simply tossed out the first one that came into his mind. "I don't know."

"But you must have some idea."

He shrugged his shoulders. "Do you know why you hate me?"

She shook her head, meaning she didn't know and didn't care to know either.

"We're even, then."

"I guess."

She asked him if it was normal for the wound on her wrist to throb.

"Yes and no," he replied, and said he'd need to take another look. She simply raised her wrist to allow him to inspect it.

He cautiously unwrapped the bandage he had made hours earlier, compared her right wrist to her left, said it wasn't swollen or red, and, cupping her wrist in one palm, asked if this hurt a bit. "You did it on purpose," she said after he had pressed the wound. He did not allow himself to answer her accusation but recommended she use the antibacterial ointment to be found in the medicine cabinet in the guest bathroom. He let go of her wrist, stood up, and was all set to walk away.

"Don't you want your bottle back?" she asked.

"Keep it." He said these words with the habitual dismissive inflection he used whenever speaking to her.

"You didn't have to hurt me, you know."

"I didn't mean to," he replied.

"Why don't I trust a thing you say?"

"I may be a complete shithead"—smirking as he used her word—"but I'm not a psycho."

She looked at him and said nothing, but it was clear she was mulling a sharp and cruel rebuke to his perfunctory apology.

"You don't think this could lead to sepsis, do you?" she finally asked.

"I've seen worse cuts."

He offered to get her the ointment. "Don't bother," she said.

"Suit yourself."

And with this he walked away.

"How is it?" he asked at breakfast the next morning.

"Better."

And this was all they said. He read the paper, she reviewed the Bach Chaconne, he spoke to his mother, she spoke to her uncle.

On the beach, when she was lying on her stomach with her bikini top off, he came up to her and, kneeling down, asked to see the cut.

"No need," she snapped.

He stood up again. "I was just offering."

"I can tell it's doing better," she replied, sensing that perhaps she had been overly brusque with him. "But take a look if you have to."

"I promise I won't touch the cut."

"And here I was looking forward to having the wound pinched, maybe even squeezed."

"I told you I wasn't a pervert."

"No, you said something else."

"I was only thinking of your word: shithead." It made the two of them laugh.

"You know," she said, "we really have no reason to hate each other. I'm not a bad person, and I'm sure you aren't either."

He decided not to argue.

"Would you do me a huge favor? Though it might totally deplete today's ration of superficial goodwill."

"What?"

"I can't use my wrist. Could you put some sunblock on my left shoulder?"

He grabbed her tube of sunblock and began rubbing her right shoulder with it.

"Wrong shoulder," she said.

"I know. I want to cover both, so you don't look ridiculous with an uneven tan. I know how important your looks are to you."

But as he was spreading the suntan lotion on her shoulders, and then on her back, he found he didn't mind touching her skin. The more he applied the cream, the slower and more lingering his hand movements.

"What are you doing?" she finally asked, sensing something different in his touch.

"Just spreading the sunblock," he replied. But then he asked her to raise herself just a tad and, without hesitating, began to apply the cream on her left breast, then her right breast. "So they don't get sunburned," he said, smiling.

She did not say anything, and simply followed with her eyes the slow, tempered motions of his palm as it caressed and kept caressing her breasts. Then, looking around at his bathing suit and sounding totally surprised, she simply said: "Oh, I see."

He did not say anything, but kept caressing one shoulder, then the other, back to the first, then to her breasts long after the cream had been spread and was fast drying on his hands. Then he reached for her tube and began applying more cream to his hands and then to the back of her neck, and to her bare back and the backs of her arms, down to her legs, her heels, and in between her toes.

"What are you doing to me?" she asked again. This time, he did not reply.

"What are you doing to me!" he finally said.

Again she looked.

Which is when she suddenly managed to lift herself, put back her bikini top as best she could with one hand, and roll up the towel she had brought with her from the house. She stood and, leaning down with her knees almost touching his chin, picked up her sunglasses, her magazines, and the tube of sunblock from his hand, and headed home. But her words—*What are you doing to me?*—wouldn't let go of him and resonated in his mind all morning as he lay stunned on the deserted beach. He suspected she was upset with him, but he also knew that, behind the veil of reproof in her words, meaning *How dare you do this to me?* her voice could have cradled an inflection of desire, astonishment, possibly surrender.

*What are you doing to me?*

No woman had said this to him before, and the strain in her voice when she'd spoken these words cast a spell that wouldn't let go of him as he lay there unable to think or read or even focus on the quiet July waves rippling to the shore. He could think of nothing but the breasts of this woman he hated. Then, almost suddenly, he realized what her words had also stirred in him, for they were neither docile nor vulnerable nor moved by anger or even passion—they were savage. She was savage—not angry, not passionate. The way she had rolled up her towel and decided to put on the bikini top despite her wrist, and exposed herself in the process without embarrassment, the way she had snubbed him after looking and smirked, was sudden, shameless, and, yes, savage.

Many hours later, when it was time for dinner, he ran into her on her way downstairs to the dining room.

Were they really going to push each other again as they'd done a few days earlier? She made a motion to let him pass by, flattening her body against the curved wall of the staircase, in a gesture that showed she was determined to avoid another shoving bout, even though both sensed that shoving, after what had happened between them on the shore, belonged to the past. But then he had done the exact same thing: by thrusting his body against the banister to let her pass, he too was suggesting that insults between them, let alone their habitual elbowing, were no longer something either wished to pursue. He read her exaggerated move to the wall as yet another instance of her overly theatrical nature, since he knew she was entirely driven by external gestures. Her reading of his own move against the banister was far more accurate. *He is nervous*, she thought. *He likes me.*

"Why did you touch me at the beach?" she asked as they proceeded down the stairs. She was expecting an answer.

Instead, she got a question: "Why did you let me?"

This did not please her, and he could tell she was about to turn mean again.

"Are we always going to be enemies?" he asked, hoping to stem the tempest before it erupted.

He had rehearsed that question and thought it was as good a way as any to bring back what had happened between them at the beach that morning.

"Are we enemies?"

With that she rushed downstairs to dinner. His heart was pounding. *We're not enemies, and she knows it.*

Just before walking into the dining room, where a guest and his wife were present, he found a moment to tell her that he couldn't believe a word of what she'd just said to him.

She smiled. "I know."

He couldn't help himself. "You know that I shouldn't believe you, or you know that I don't?"

She looked at him again the way she'd just done, and repeated: "I told you, I know."

No one in his life had puzzled him so. Everyone else he'd met was transparent, even when they tried to remain elusive.

"Do I scare you so much that you need to speak to me in riddles?"

She thought for a moment before greeting one of the guests.

"It's not you I'm scared of."

"Of whom then?"

"*Of whom then*," she mimicked. "It's me I'm scared of. Me. You understand?"

He was totally baffled.

"Now you know."

Not a word between them throughout the dinner. Afterward, she managed to catch him on his way upstairs.

"I'll come to your room."

"When?" he asked.

"I don't know."

That night he could not sleep. Each time anything in the house creaked, he was sure that she was opening his door. But then he realized that she was not the furtive type to go about the house on tiptoes, to open doors softly. Besides, he had left his door ajar, something he'd never done before, precisely to let her know she was welcome in. Why hadn't she come, then? Perhaps she had made her promise on the fly and had just meant to tease him, with never a thought of going through with it. Or perhaps something he had said right after dinner had made her change her mind. Or had she simply fallen asleep and forgotten?

Sensing she wasn't coming, he resolved to make himself dream of her, and perhaps he did dream, though it wasn't exactly a dream, but just like a dream, during which all he did was revisit over and over again what she meant at the beach when she'd said *What are you doing?* and moments later, once he'd rubbed her breasts and begun to massage her feet, the heel, the arch, and then the toes and in between the toes of each foot, he'd heard *What are you doing to me?* And in his dream, all he replied was *You know exactly what I'm doing, of course you know, you've always known.* And then came the moment he savored most but kept postponing each time he saw it coming from the periphery of his dreaming mind and enjoyed deferring as much as he could so as to arrive at it after many delays—the moment that he knew had happened when she had suddenly turned before standing up to leave the beach. Oh, she'd seen, all right, and he liked that she'd seen, how couldn't she have, because this too was true about the two of them: they cared for each other so little as to harbor no shame, no qualms, nothing to hold them back, which is why he had touched her and why she'd let him, and why she'd seen and he was pleased that she had.

"You never came last night," he said to her the next morning.

"Did I say I would?"

"I just wish you had."

"I never apologize."

He refused to speak to her. When he went to the beach later that day, he made a point of lying far away from her.

But then one morning, after he'd resolved never to give her another thought, he woke up and found her sitting on his desk chair staring at him.

"How long have you been there?"

"A while."

"Just staring at me sleeping?"

"Yes."

"Why?"

"Because I can learn so much about someone by watching him sleep."

"What did you learn?"

"I learned that you can be a very sweet man, but your sleep is not happy. You clench your jaw and you look angry sometimes, as though fighting demons."

"Maybe I was thinking of you then."

Realizing what he'd just said, he felt he needed to say more: "All I do is think of you. I go to sleep thinking of you, dream of you, and wake up with this." He wanted to shock her. She wasn't shocked.

"Seriously?" she said.

"And then one day I open my eyes and I find you in my bedroom." He moved to the side of his bed and lifted the sheet again, clearly inviting her to his bed.

"No," she said.

She did not know why she'd said *no* so gruffly, but she also enjoyed turning him down.

"You don't trust me?"

"I already told you. It's not you I don't trust." And having said this, she left his room.

But a few nights later, he didn't have long to think before deciding to slip into her bedroom. Not knowing what to wear, he decided to put on his bathing suit. Her clothes were lying on a chair, so he sat on a low wooden cabinet that housed the family's sewing machine and simply watched her sleep, even though it was getting colder by dawn.

"What are you doing?" she said when she finally opened her eyes.

"It's my turn," he said.

She did not say anything, just looked at him and at his bathing suit. "Were you planning to swim in my bedroom?"

They both laughed.

"I haven't decided. But I'm cold and this swimming suit at this hour is utterly ridiculous. I didn't know what to wear."

"Aren't you cold?"

"Freezing."

Using her feet, she pushed her sheet away and exposed her naked body. "I've been thinking of you."

She didn't have to add another word. He removed his bathing suit and, shivering, crawled into her bed. She hugged him, kept him warm with the weight of her body, and, placing the palm of her hands on each side of his face, said, "I'm so glad you came."

From that moment on, as if under a spell, the two were as inseparable as Tristan and Iseult.

What neither realized was that all their bile and venom and their contempt for each other was precisely what allowed instant intimacy to spread between them without their sensing, much less suspecting, that it had already happened. It didn't flourish, it didn't blossom, it simply sprang on them that day on the beach when he'd thrown his water bottle next to her on the sand and then touched her skin. Because neither even thought, much less wished, there could be anything between them, they let their bodies decide, not their hearts, not their minds, not even the thrill of secrecy from everyone in the household. For all they knew, their one night together was going to happen once, and once only. But it was because they expected nothing, not even pleasure, that they couldn't let go of each other. This, as she, the Bach student, explained one day, was intimacy by *contrario motu*. They backed into each other's life and spent the remainder of that summer making love every moment they could. They never asked why they made love, but they made love without holding back, because, at least at first, neither seemed to care what the other thought, or felt, or needed. What cleared their way was not friendship; it was enmity that fooled them.

They lasted four months, until October. She wanted to give up Oxford, he wanted to follow her there. They were smart enough to know that nothing lasts, least of all fiery passion—but they lay naked every morning on their rock, they made love every afternoon and every night, and sometimes they'd end up at the movies, interested in nothing and no one except each other. There wasn't a thing they didn't do together. She once asked him if this was real. "Does any of it not feel real?" he'd answered. "No." "So why ask?" "Because we need to ask, because we need to know, because I fear the worst." "If you're going to England, I want to be on the same plane with you. If you're ever on a boat, I want to sail on it. If you're crossing the street, even, I'll walk with you."

She died in a car accident not five miles away. She had just turned twenty-two. There was bad light that night, the twisting roads along the cliff were slippery and the fog dense. He should have stopped her. Something told him, though, the moment he remembered that they had never once, not once, used the word *love*. That's how he suddenly knew that something was amiss. The thought wouldn't have come to him otherwise. But he didn't trust himself and chose to overlook the signs.

"I can do many things," Raúl said. "I can cure someone's back pain, let kidney stones dissolve into nothing, make tempests happen, stop boats from sailing. When I was a boy, I could make the school bus arrive late at school, have parking spaces suddenly materialize so my father wouldn't get upset, even have the food ready long before we stepped into a restaurant or had even ordered. But this was beyond me."

He was quiet for a moment.

"'One day,' I told her, 'we could lose interest in whatever we have and be back to hating each other—ramming each other up and down the stairwell.' 'But then,' she said, 'I'll hurt myself and you'll tend to my cut and before we know it, you'll slip into my bedroom wearing that swimsuit, asking to be kept warm, and we'll swim out to our rock and make love there till dawn catches us freezing.'"

"Do I remind you of her? Were you thinking of making love to me when we were on the rock together?" Margot asked.

"You don't understand."

"What don't I understand?"

"I did make love to you on the rock. Except . . ."

"Except?"

"Except it was forty years ago. Her name, as I'm sure you've guessed by now, was Marya. But looking back now, it was I who died, not she, I who've been dead my whole life, except . . ."

"Except, again?"

"Except she is you, and you are more alive today than I've ever been."

Margot heard him say this and bristled. It made her entire life feel like a fraud, as though her life as Marya, if indeed it was a previous life, took precedence over everything she'd lived, known, and done. She wasn't prepared to accept this shadow-self, she said.

"Please don't be angry with me. It was not my intention to belittle your current life, or to ask the previous one to compete with it, or take it over. All I wanted was to be with you—for a few hours, for a few days, that's all." He paused. "Before we leave this house, which you may never want to see again, at least not with me and certainly not when I'm alive, I want to show you something."

"What?" she asked. By now she'd grown restless and hostile.

He did not tell her what. Instead, he led her up the stairs to the first floor—"This is the famous stairway," he said—and then up to the second floor. He opened the door to a small room.

"I know the smell of that room," she said. "I know that smell."

"It was once your room. You do know what stood here, on this very spot." He could tell that she had already guessed or, rather, had always known. She did not have to say.

"Correct," he replied. "And I want you to see this," he said, opening a closet. "We initially saved it as a keepsake. But I kept it, knowing you'd be back to see it one day." He took it out of its case, then unwrapped its felt covering.

"May I?" she asked, meaning to touch it.

"It's yours. You can take it now, if you wish."

"Seriously?" she asked as she rubbed a palm delicately on its glistening maple back.

"Very seriously."

"But I've never played."

He smiled.

"But why are you giving it to me?"

"It's the only proof I have that you are who you are, that you are back. You see, you didn't die, you just went away."

"I can't take it."

"Well, think about it. Promise? It's yours."

She nodded.

"I also want to show you something else," he said.

"What now?"

He ignored her tone and opened another door, which revealed a linen closet. He put his hand under a thin sheet of cloth lining one of the tiny shelves filled with folded tablecloths and colored napkins and pulled out a square envelope from underneath. He opened the unsealed envelope and produced a colored snapshot of a young man and a young woman wearing bathing suits. They're both smiling broadly and squinting a bit, probably because of the sun in their faces. In the distance lies the rock. She is holding a plastic bag while attempting to hide it behind her back. Her hair is short, the two of them are very tanned.

"Marya?" Margot asked.

"Marya," he replied.

"She looks like me."

"She is you."

"We even have the same knees, and the same feet."

"Same elbows," he added, as she raised her elbows to take a better look at them.

She agreed.

"The two of you look so alike," she said.

"I know. Sometimes we felt we were the same person."

"So, you've kept this photo."

"Of course I've kept it. It's the only picture I have of the two of us."

"Who took the picture?"

"Someone."

"What's in the plastic bag that she's trying to hide from the picture?"

"You know the answer. Fruit. She'd just rinsed it in seawater."

Again Margot stared at the picture.

"Take it," said Raúl.

"I can't take it. It's yours."

"It means more to me now if you take it. Plus . . ."

"I hate when you do this. Plus what?"

"There's a reason why I want you to have it." He waited a few seconds. "I want you to remember the face of the young man in the picture."

"Why?"

"You'll meet him when you're my age."

"You make the rest of my life feel so joyless, so totally pointless." She gave what she'd just said some thought. "Just take me back to our hotel."

Together they left the room and walked down the old stairwell.

## Chapter Six

On their way, she walked much faster than they'd done earlier, either in a rush to get back to the hotel or determined now to show that she was keeping her distance. He was not surprised. She had to shower and change, she said. Her friends were planning a night out at one of the clubs in the hills. He bade her good evening and they separated in the lobby as she entered the elevator—but then suddenly she stepped out again. All manner of hopes raced through his mind when he saw her exit so swiftly, and he was sure he had totally misjudged her. With a simple gesture, she removed the sweater and gave it back to him before rushing into the elevator.

Later, when he walked into the dining area to his usual table by the illuminated pool, her friends hailed him.

"Malcolm was asking if you had any more tips for him," said Basil.

"All out of tips tonight. Send him my apologies."

Oscar showed him his new hat. "My newest conquest."

Raúl congratulated him. "And the shoulder?" he asked Mark.

"Couldn't be better."

She did not greet him, but continued to chat with Angelica; nor did she even turn to look at him, though he knew she was aware of his presence at the table, where barely a few hours earlier he'd had one of his happiest lunches in so many years. Strange, he thought, she didn't use to be so chatty with everyone, and now she was all ebullient and sprightly, talking to Oscar, to Mr. January, Miss May, and Mr. November, far across their table. *I've lost her. For the second time in my life, I've lost her.* There was a moment when they were lying on the rock together like the most intimate of lovers, friends, *âmes sœurs.* He knew that she'd felt it as well, that moment. But life can take the most perfect day and ruin it. If life doesn't do it, then we'll be the ones to do it. This now, he could tell, was indeed ruined.

On her way out of the dining area, she passed by his table and stopped short right by the chair where she'd sat during lunch. With her he didn't want to know anything or anticipate what she was going to say. He wanted her to sit at his table and pick up where they'd left off at lunch. Instead, she just stood before him, even placed a hand on the tablecloth, but said nothing. She looked so pinched that he knew she was mulling over how to strafe him with a volley of cutting words.

But she wasn't saying anything: she was waiting for the others to leave the area before talking to him; but even after they'd left she still wasn't speaking. He simply looked up at her beautiful face; he too had nothing to say. "You could have warned me about the car that night, you could have warned me. Why didn't you?"

"Because I didn't believe it could happen. Because I thought I was being unreasonably paranoid. Because I just didn't want to think of it."

"You didn't want to think of it. That's some gem, Raúl."

She tapped her knuckles on his table twice, as if to drive her point home. But she wasn't leaving yet. "And for your information," she added, "I still remember the accident. I remember the sound in the car and the sound of the bones breaking in my body, and I remember not dying right away too."

He sat silent.

"Oh, and one more thing," she added. "It was not the road, not the fog, not the swirling eddies of rain that kept buffeting the hood of our car. Your driver was drunk. You hired a drunk driver. Why hadn't you told me?"

"I wish I'd died with you in the same car," he said. "We'd have been spared all this. Now we have to wait."

"Oh, please!" With that she hurriedly pulled on her windbreaker and, hearing the call of her friends, who had ordered three cars, was about to walk out when she turned back to Raúl. "So tell me now, should I get in the car, you think?"

He smiled at her. "Yes, it's safe."

"Good night, then."

"Good night," he said.

He didn't quite understand what she'd meant by asking about the ride. Was she pulling his leg and making light of his prophetic powers? He wasn't even able to interpret the word *then* that she'd just used. Was it an amicable, conciliatory *then* that came like a friendly nudge of the elbow after strong words? Or did it underscore the chill, ironic cloud between them, and, as always with her, something unavoidably hostile and dismissive?

She had left the dining hall with peremptory haste, but a few moments later she returned. "And one more thing: if you had anything to do with our boat, maybe it's time you released it."

She had given everything he'd said a great deal of thought. That bit about their boat, which he'd thrown in as an afterthought when talking about kidney stones and back pains, hadn't escaped her. *So, you understand everything then*, he thought of saying to her. He heard the cars leave the hotel and feared he'd never see her again.

That night, he did what he'd done so many nights before. He took out a cigarette, found himself a chair and a table, ordered a strong drink, and sat down and smoked. Nothing to read—he didn't really want to be distracted; nothing to listen to—music would blur his thoughts. He just wanted to think of the young man who'd entered a girl's room in his bathing suit and sat there, waiting for her to wake up and share the warmth of her body.

The cigarette took forever to smoke. Then, at some point, he decided to stub it out, finished his drink, and opted for a walk along the shore. He left his glasses on the table, removed his shoes, rolled his trousers, and proceeded to walk to the beach. Isn't this what those who are about to take their own lives do when they leave a note in their shoes on the edge of a bridge? Why on earth do people remove their shoes but not their socks, he thought, and what about their wallets, their watch—why punish a watch that stayed loyal to you all life long?

It made him want to laugh. He heard himself snickering.

What he couldn't quite fathom was why she had become so angry the closer he got to the truth. The more he convinced her she was Marya, the more she bristled. The violin was hers, so why hadn't she taken it, now that she knew he hadn't lied, now that she recalled the accident, recalled the sound of the car tumbling down, with the sound of her body breaking, and the drunk driver whose body, so they said, fell not just out of the car but down into the sea, never to be recovered? *Se l'hanno mangiato i pesci*, the fish ate him, they said. But he couldn't let go of the moment when she had come up to his table, placed a palm on the tablecloth and asked why he hadn't warned her of the accident, as if it had all been his fault, and to bring the point home, had rapped the table twice. He'd never forget that gesture, followed by a smiling *then*, as if she'd meant no harm, as if peace were never in doubt between them, as if war and peace were, in the end, identical bedfellows.

Then there was that other instant, when she had swum with him to the rock and he had helped her up there with him. What a beautiful moment—one to make the gods envious.

Of course they were envious.

That night, the walk on the shore took him to the spot where the old lighthouse used to stand. He saw it now not as he remembered or as Alberti had captured it less than a decade after the war, but as she had described it: *a squat little hut made of stacked boulders with a strange round attic-looking structure from which scant light emanated to warn mariners of rocks and shoals.* Her words. Exactly as in the photo. Later, when he was back in his room, a strange thought kept buzzing in his mind. He was pleased that they had spent time together, yet, on second thought, now that they'd been together, there was little left for him to do. He had waited so long for this, and now it had come and gone—come and gone, he repeated to himself.

*Come and gone*, he whispered the words to himself as he brushed his teeth a while later, *come and gone*, as he read a few pages before sensing he was about to doze off, *come and gone*, when he was finally about to turn off his bedside light and thought about his own life that had come six decades ago and would soon be gone. *And why not*, he thought. *And why not.*

Then he heard the knock at his door. *I knew it, I've always known*, he thought.

"Come in."

She was dressed in exactly the clothes she'd been wearing when she'd stood before him and placed a hand on his table. Same blouse, same sweater, same necklace, same way she'd arranged her hair. Only her lipstick had faded.

"Finish the story," she said, removing her linen shawl and sitting on the armchair that was close to his bed. He made a motion to turn on the main light in the room, but she told him not to.

"The story," he said, with a melancholy smile. "They wouldn't let me see the body. A few days later they wanted to take away her things and her clothes, but I didn't let them.

"Everything in her room stayed the way she left it. When I revisit the town, I always make a point of going upstairs and stepping into her room; I'll sit on her bed, think of her. There were times when I've flown all the way from Peru to sleep in her bed. Those are the only times in my life when I sleep so soundly. Sometimes I speak to her, sometimes I imagine what she'd say. 'I've grown so old,' I'll say. 'Yes, you've grown old, and you do look old, my dear, dear man,' she replies. And I'll ask her if she remembers the rock, or the cut on her wrist, or the sewing machine, and she'll say she still does, of course she does. And yet we never used the word *love*."

"Why is that?"

"Maybe because it was more than just love, or maybe it was something else. But it never went away, and I don't want it to. Still today, that one sentence she spoke to me some forty years ago—*Were you planning to swim in my bedroom?*—brings a smile to my life."

Raúl couldn't see her, she sat slightly behind him, and he liked it that way. There was a moment, given the silence that suddenly hovered between them, when he felt that perhaps she had already slipped away and left his room, or had never even been there.

"Why did you come tonight?" he asked.

"Because you wanted me to. Because I really didn't want us to drift away. Because I could tell you weren't happy, especially after such a lovely day."

"So now we read minds?"

"I had a good teacher. But finish the story," she said, as he heard her move the armchair closer to his bed.

He told her that he'd always kept an eye on her as she was growing up, had tried not to intrude, but knew where she lived, which school she attended, what college she was applying to, who her friends and roommates were. He kept hoping she'd pick up the violin, but she never did. "And, honestly, part of me was waiting for you to get older."

"Older than Marya?"

"Yes, otherwise I doubt you'd have spoken to me, much less had lunch with me."

He turned around and saw that she was shaking her head slightly, as if to reproach him for something she had no words for, so just the gesture would do.

"Why not let go of me, forget, let the whole thing just go?"

"Can I now, especially after today? Can you?"

"I'm going to try."

"Don't you think I've tried? Do you have any idea how happy you've made me? Mine wasn't bereavement. I wasn't in mourning. I wasn't even sad you died. I was just missing half my body, half my life, maybe all of it. I ended up living another man's life, not mine. I was no longer me. And yet I was a master at faking it with everyone. For years, each time I was alone—in the shower, or getting dressed, or in bed, or in the kitchen cutting up vegetables on a Sunday evening—I'd mutter your name, *Mar-a-ya*, out loud and feel completely ridiculous doing so, and yet I was still happy that this name had come into my life, that I could call it, and by calling it even talk to it, as I'm talking to you now. At some point I realized that I just had to see you. Not to relive what had happened four decades before. All I wanted was to have you with me, for an hour, for a day—more I never dreamed of asking."

"And?"

"I could have waited more time, as I'd been doing for so long, letting another five weeks, five months, five years, go by. But my time's almost up, and this now is the hardest part for me, telling you what lies in store for me. For me the matter will be settled soon enough. I laugh at what awaits me: new parents, new schooling, new siblings, and the years and years of our crossing paths and never stopping, or occasionally turning back to catch a second glimpse only to let go because it's not our time, not our time yet, never our time."

"How many years, Raúl?"

This was the first time she'd used his name. It pleased him and it moved him.

"How many? I don't want to tell you."

"Why not?"

"Too many."

"Just tell me."

He hesitated for a moment.

"Three hundred and twenty-four. Eighteen times eighteen years."

"Will we keep missing each other?"

"One day, when you're old and gray, you'll see a young man step out of a car, or walk into your hotel lobby, or enter a concert hall, and you'll say, I know him, he's the man I met years ago at that hotel in southern Italy who kept telling me he'd known me another lifetime ago. It will be the young man in the picture, which is why I wanted you to keep it. I too will again and again run into you, but I'll be too old or too young, or you'll be too old or too young. But that day will come, I promise, though I have no vision of what our planet will be like."

"I hate goodbyes, especially after today. You make me fear the years of loneliness awaiting me. Or worse yet, that my life and eighteen generations of my life will mean nothing. What do I do with these lifetimes? No one can wait this long."

"We are all of us condemned to loneliness, each and every one of us. You died alone. I'll die alone. You yelled my name when the car fell, I call out yours each and every night of my life. At some point fate will realign our calendars, and if we're lucky, we'll live seventy long years together and then never again."

He knew he was tearing up and so he stopped talking.

"Any idea what a privilege it was to have you for two

lunches, to walk with you in the sun, to swim with you and let myself dream I was a young man again, eating fruit on the rock by the old lighthouse that isn't even there any longer?"

"What had you hoped might happen to us?" she asked.

"Nothing. I wanted you to love the young man I once was. I wanted you to look at me and tell me that you'd forgotten nothing, that you'd suffered for forty-plus years without knowing you were suffering, that you couldn't have been more grateful I'd brought you back here."

"Did you really have something to do with the boat?" she asked.

"Yes," he replied.

"Will you let it go?"

"When do you want me to?"

"Friday. This gives us two days."

"Two more lunches, two more walks to our beach, the rock, maybe the house again." Then he asked, because he had to ask: "Will you be on the boat when I let it go?"

"I don't know. Yes. No. I don't know."

"You will have to be. But tomorrow, very early, I'd planned a small errand for us."

"An errand?"

"I want to take you to the cemetery. I want you to see her grave. And, as in the poem, we'll bring a nosegay of green holly and heather blossom."

"Because?"

"Because it will be my way of closing the circle. At the very last minute you will go back with your friends and perhaps not believe a word of what happened here and, looking back, call the whole thing an old man's bluff, an old man's fiction. But seeing the grave will etch me forever in your heart. I've loved only you and will continue to love you long, long after I'm gone. In the years to come I want you to return, most likely with your husband, your children, or come alone—yes, come alone. I don't have descendants, so the house will be yours. I signed over the deed three days ago. Only promise me one thing. Bury me near her."

He turned to her. "Aren't you cold?" he finally asked.

"Freezing," she replied.

He remembered that word.

He'd waited a lifetime to hear her say it.

# ROOM ON THE SEA

## Monday

He was reading the newspaper. She was reading a novel. He looked at her once. She did not look back. She had fair hair, which was combed to the side, and from the way she held her book and rested it on the knee of her crossed leg, he could tell she had the hands of a pianist. He attempted to catch the title of her novel but was unable to make it out. When she turned the page, he tried once more but failed again. Moments later, he made one last try. "It's *Wuthering Heights*," she whispered so as not to disturb the others seated in the large hall. She appeared mildly amused by his curiosity, and to prove that her novel was no secret, she turned the book cover for him to see for himself, thinking perhaps that he'd probably never heard of it. He was not sure why he needed to know what she was reading other than because he'd kept failing each time or because, without quite admitting it to himself, he was trying to make conversation. But after showing him the title of her novel, she went back to reading and was seemingly more absorbed than before. "Actually, I've read it twice," he said. "In school, we used to call it *Weather and Heights*." She thought that was amusing and emitted a quiet, breathless laugh, more out of courtesy than because it was funny. "It's a tired old joke," he added, "but it holds up if you've never heard it before." This time she gave a perfunctory smile, did not say anything, and continued reading. He went back to his *Wall Street Journal.*

She was dressed in light linen with her shoulders exposed on that hot summer Monday but had brought a cotton sweater just in case the air-conditioning made the central jury room unbearably cold. But the air-conditioning wasn't working in the large hall, where at least two hundred people were bunched together waiting to be selected as jurors. Eventually, at nine thirty, the jury warden picked up his microphone, welcomed everyone, and, with a touch of mirth in his voice, apologized for the cooling system, reminding those present that the heat was just as intolerable to those working in the building as it was to prospective jurors. Everyone seemed grateful for the humor, and a muted chuckle rippled through the hall.

Meanwhile, the man put down his *Journal,* removed his striped blue worsted wool jacket, and laid it, neatly folded in two, on the seat between them. He thought of loosening his necktie and unbuttoning the top of his shirt but decided not to. Before making his passing remark on *Weather and Heights,* he had started to undo his thick gold cuff links, shaped like a marine chain, which now dangled at his wrists. His shoes were shimmering black brogues, the kind her husband never wore. His black socks did not droop; her husband's did. Jonathan never cared if his socks bunched up around his ankles, but this dapper man most likely wore garters around his calves. She could read him like a book: Wall Street, Park Avenue, Ivy League—arrogant, self-satisfied, clearly prejudiced, and knows it too.

They stayed glued to their reading until his name was called out: Paul Wadsworth. Of course, she thought. He was ordered to take the elevator to Part 73. "Enjoy your reading," he said, picking up his jacket and cuffing his sleeves again with the visible ease of someone who, unlike Jonathan, never needed help with cuff links. "Emily Brontë beats the *Journal* hands down," he added.

"I couldn't agree more," she replied.

Definitely lefty, he thought, an opinionated and dismissive Upper West Side liberal who deplored his sort.

He left the main waiting hall and made his way to the courtroom. He seated himself on one of the benches and waited to be called. The lawyers were discussing matters among themselves. Meanwhile, the door behind him opened and he turned around to notice that another group of jurors was being ushered in. She was among them. He noticed that her hair was not dirty blond, as he first thought when they were seated in the central jury room, but an attractive, shiny gray. She caught his glance and rushed to his spot, finding an empty seat right behind him. Leaning forward, she asked: "Do you have a way out of this?"

"I think I do," he replied.

"Please tell me what it is. I can't afford to be here. Any advice?"

He stood up, grabbed his newspaper, cleared his way to the aisle, and found a spot next to her. "Two things," he said, lowering his voice. "What exasperates lawyers most when they voir dire you is being answered with a straight yes or no, not a single syllable more. They'll figure you're either a lawyer or have some experience with the bench and suspect you'll see right through their legal shenanigans. I'm wearing a lawyer's suit—they know why, and they know I know why. Basically, they'll know I'm a lawyer, and they don't want a lawyer controlling the jury room during deliberations. As for you, don't volunteer anything. Just a simple yes or no.

"Now, since this is criminal court they'll ask if you've ever been the victim of a crime. They might give you a chance to elaborate on one such incident. In the past, I told them the truth: I've had no experience with crime, but I'll add that my mother was mugged at gunpoint while she stood at the cash register in a supermarket. This will most probably please the prosecution. But then I'll remind the judge that the police did not pay attention to a word she said when they arrived at the scene. Because she spoke with a foreign accent, the officers proved so hostile to her that she lost all respect for them and refused to file a report. 'Can you be impartial?' the judge will ask. 'Honestly, Your Honor, I don't know, but I'll try my best.' It's worked twice in the recent past. Both the defense and prosecution felt uncertain about me and didn't want me as a juror."

As it turned out, when his turn came, he did as he had told her he would and was summarily dismissed and sent back to the central jury room. He took out his copy of *The Wall Street Journal* and picked up where he had left off before being called to the courtroom. When, after more than an hour, he saw that she wasn't coming back, he figured she must have fumbled her reply to one or both lawyers, and had, as a result, been impaneled.

But no. Fifteen minutes after he'd given up, the elevator bell rang and she appeared in the main hall. She looked around, spotted him, and walked straight up to him.

"It worked!" She was beaming like a child.

"Don't tell anyone I told you."

"Of course I won't."

"It's a well-kept secret. You know," he added, removing his jacket from the empty seat next to him to make room for her, "I once told someone about a hotel in Naples where I always stayed because of an important client I had there. The hotel was not particularly pretty, but one room was heavenly. 'Ask for room 68B and none other,' I said. Well, ever since that day, the rumor must have spread like wildfire among people in my line, because I could no longer book that same room. I eventually found a better hotel with a better view of the city—of the shoreline and Mount Vesuvius. But now mum's the word."

"In my business," she said, "we know how to keep secrets."

"What's your business?" he asked, feeling he could already guess.

"Basically a headshrinker," she replied with a slight giggle and a touch of meekness verging on an apology for her profession. The word *headshrinker* fell like an old punch line to a joke that's been retold too many times to need an intro. Then, with a touch of boldness that almost surprised him: "What's the name of the hotel?"

"Its name is Albergo Segreto, i.e., the Secret Hotel."

She pondered the answer. "Oh!" she finally exclaimed. "So you're not going to tell me?" There was an affected, slighted pout to her voice. He liked how she pretended to reproach him without meaning to.

"I'll tell you, but not before you explain what you told the judge."

As it turned out, she hadn't made up a story for the judge. Her daughter, walking with her four-year-old son, had been robbed in plain sight on Columbus Avenue. She had right away called 911, and when the police came they asked her to describe the perpetrator. She had been so flustered and so frightened for her child that she hadn't focused on the criminal and was unable to describe him to the police. They told her to come to the precinct to file a report. "But by then the mugger will have disappeared," she'd objected. "Lady," said one of the two officers, with a cheeky, all-knowing smile on his face, obviously enjoying what he was about to tell her, "your mugger disappeared long, long ago." *Your mugger* stuck in her craw. Like his mother, she refused to file a report. She was more furious with the officers than with the mugger.

By then it was nearing twelve forty-five and the jury was allowed an hour and a half for lunch. They had to be back by two fifteen sharp, said the warden on the PA system.

So they rushed out. He said he knew of a Chinese restaurant close by that served very fast and quite decent food. She loved the idea. Oh, she exclaimed, almost taking a step back, did he mind if she tagged along? Absolutely not. Was he really a lawyer? "Yes. What makes you ask?" "The look," she replied, grazing his lapel with her palm and almost laughing at the wool suit on such a hot day. He'd retired the year before but hadn't quite gotten used to life as a former partner. He still had an office on Pearl Street, though he'd grown to like working from home.

Did he like what he did?

"Yes. Mostly. Sometimes. Frankly, seldom," he said, laughing for the first time at his disclosure. She liked how he laughed. He was not the stuffy investment banker type that she'd imagined. Knew how to make fun of himself—not too much, but just enough to pass her tentative sense-of-humor test, which she applied when judging patients and people in general.

How about her, he asked, did she like being a shrink?

"*Mostly. Sometimes. Frankly, seldom*," she said, echoing his very words, perhaps also meaning to pull his leg. Then, fearing she'd gone overboard: "Honestly, I do like being a shrink." But her defense was underscored by an indecisive note. With an unstated *maybe* in her voice, she added that she sometimes nursed second thoughts about her career, especially at this late stage of the game. She had even thought of possibly retiring. "But then what would I do with myself all day?" Besides, she'd never own up to any of this to anyone, and certainly not to a stranger. "But then why am I telling you all this?"

"Most likely because I am a stranger, and you're free to say anything you please."

She said he didn't strike her as the combative lawyer type.

"That's because I have always avoided litigation. I never go to court, I have others do that. I turn out to be right in my assessment of most cases, yet there is always a part of me that fears being wrong. Retirement was the very best thing I did as a lawyer. Think about it."

Both liked that neither wished to sound too self-satisfied with their career. They also tried their best not to pry into each other's lives. It gave their walk together a light, laid-back, casual cast, which they enjoyed.

"Oh, and by the way, my name is Catherine."

He couldn't resist: "Call me Heathcliff."

They laughed as they entered one of the crowded Chinese restaurants less than ten minutes away from the courthouse.

Lunch was fast and fun. Neither knew quite what the other liked. Did she mind cilantro? he asked. No, but her husband did. "He hates the taste."

"That's so strange, my wife hates cilantro too. I read somewhere that there are people who cannot stand cilantro because it reminds them of Ivory Soap. We never order Chinese food."

"Neither do we."

"Strange world, isn't it."

"Strange, indeed, and yet here we are about to."

Both laughed again, though each wondered if the other had caught the reason for their laughter. It might have been an unintended, tacit dig at the lives they lived, but it could just as easily have been the sheer coincidence of having spouses with identical taste buds.

The soup was wonderful, the fried dumplings the best she'd had in years, and the prawn and the chicken-cashew plates, both of which they felt relaxed enough to share, were beyond delicious. Yesterday's chicken and last night's soup, but who cares! he said. She agreed. The unidentified leftover, a culinary secret all its own, she added.

Did he cook? All the time, in the past. Did she? Seldom. Her husband was picky and didn't like her in the kitchen when he was preparing dinner. So she learned not to meddle, though she did like cooking. Did they cook together? she asked. His wife complained he got too many pots and dishes dirty, given the few items he ended up preparing, especially now that there were only the two of them left, as their sons were married and living elsewhere.

Life, he said with a light chuckle. Life indeed, she repeated.

When they left the restaurant, they had a good half hour before heading back to the central jury room.

"Coffee?" he suggested.

"Absolutely."

The walk took three minutes. Da Pirro bar-café-enoteca, which he said all young lawyers in his firm raved about, was crowded. They had to wait in line, heard the people before them order all manner of convoluted coffees, and when their turn came, paying took more time than having their coffee poured.

"I feel that we're on a strange countdown," she said.

"I know. We have fifteen minutes left, minus the five for being screened through the metal detector and then heading upstairs on the crawling elevators."

He said he liked a hot coffee on a hot day—go figure! She said she hated chunks of ice in hers.

"Can we at least disagree on something?" he asked, knowing she'd appreciate the humor.

"I'm sure we'll find something if we meet again," she joked, then, fearing he might take her comment the wrong way, she added something to suggest that jury duty might last longer than either of them wished. He couldn't agree more, he said.

"There was a time when lawyers were immediately dismissed. Now they are still dismissed but they have to serve time first, like everyone else. Honestly, though, this was truly enjoyable."

She agreed with him, and as they walked out into the glaring noonday sun holding their to-go cups, she turned to him and said, "This has been a happy day for me."

He nodded to show that he'd heard and registered what she'd just said. They stood waiting for the crosswalk light to change, and, sensing that an awkward silence was about to settle between them, she added: "Sometimes a random moment occurs, and then you realize that it came with a small halo." This time he looked at her and nodded once more. It allowed her to say, "Well, I just wanted to say the bold, unadorned something before it gets all clumsy and foiled and then goes into hiding. So thank you," she said.

"My pleasure," he replied, which is what he told so many after dispensing legal advice. But then, sensing that *my pleasure* was a touch too vacuous after what she'd just said to him and could easily pass for a bland *you're welcome*: "If it felt special it's probably because none of it was planned. You helped put the halo too."

"Take the credit!" she reproached with a soft laugh. "I would have bought a bagel with cream cheese and sat like a widow on one of those park benches, kicking the pigeons away."

"With any luck, we might do this again tomorrow."

"With any luck."

They were separated within five minutes of returning. She was sent to Part 81, he to 66.

As he picked up his jacket and draped it across his arm, he couldn't help blurting out, "We may never see each other again."

"I know."

It occurred to both, without knowing why, that something dismayed them in the separation. They hadn't expected to feel this way, which is why neither had time to conceal it.

"Life," he said once more, shrugging his shoulders philosophically. He wasn't sure she'd heard him. It didn't matter.

But on his way up on the elevator, he suddenly remembered that Heathcliff wasn't his name, Heathcliff was a joke, just a silly, stupid, stupid joke. What an idiot!

*A lovely man*, she thought. Then she regretted not telling him that. She liked how he had opened up to her about his job and then, in passing, told her that his wife complained he got too many dishes dirty in the kitchen. *Still, I bet they're the kind who drink wine together while cooking at night. We don't.*

As he was being questioned by the defense attorney, he fumbled with his answers, even argued with the lawyer on the appropriateness of the question he was asked, was chided by the presiding judge but summarily released by the defense. Without intending it, he had acted the part of a crazy person. *They don't mind fools in the jury box, but no crazies*, he thought.

When he was back in the main hall, he saw that others were seated at his and her seats and that she was gone. *Teaches me to use a nickname.* He knew it was pointless to try to find her. This time she'd probably managed to get herself impaneled. He went back to scanning his paper. He hadn't touched it since they'd spoken.

If she'd been impaneled, he'd have lunch alone on the morrow. He didn't mind having lunch alone. Lunch alone had never upset him—so long as those sitting in front of him didn't slurp their soup or champ their food too loudly. *Ours was*, he thought, *a tiny, fleeting episode in a Chinese restaurant near the courts.* No, not an episode, just a nice little fleeting moment—he didn't know how else to describe it. A moment. Then he remembered and smiled. A small halo, she'd called it.

He was still reading the headlines in his paper when he heard, "A penny for them." He didn't recognize the voice behind him. A friend, or an old colleague, a friend of a friend, maybe a neighbor, who was also on jury duty?

He turned around to see.

"How quickly we forget," she said, noticing the deft and hasty cover-up of what had been a vacant look clouding his features.

He realized that he had unintentionally played a little trick on himself. He had refused to believe that the person speaking to him was the very one he had wished to see again. He was thrilled and he told her so.

"I almost bashed my head against the elevator door for giving you a stupid name."

"How silly did you think I was? I knew Heathcliff wasn't yours. You are Paul Wadsworth. You responded to it when they called you out this morning."

He, on the other hand, had never caught her full name. Catherine Shukoff, she said.

She took the seat next to him. Neither was going to read. There were many things they wanted to say, but they were so surprised to find each other that they couldn't think of one. Or maybe they had already depleted everything at lunch and all that remained were meager residuals that wouldn't have lasted more than a minute or two. What made further reflections irrelevant was the sudden announcement on the PA system, apologizing for the intense heat both outside and inside the courthouse. "Meaning?" cried one of the outspoken people in the hall. "Meaning," replied the person on the PA system, not without a snicker in his voice, "that you are released for the day, but must be back tomorrow morning at nine thirty sharp," adding, "I know how disappointed you must all be."

There was buoyant laughter in the hall. Within seconds everyone stood up and was hastily vacating the room, just like pupils who've been released from school on the announcement of summer break.

"I'll bring coffee for the two of us," he said.

"And I'll bring the croissants."

"Better idea—let's meet at Da Pirro tomorrow, before the court opens. They won't allow us to bring coffee inside the court."

"Done."

He was going to walk to his office, she was taking the Eighth Avenue to the Upper Shrink Side. She thought it was funny the way they rushed out of the hall the moment they heard the announcer say that he was sure they were all utterly disappointed. Paul emitted something like a laugh.

Then they said goodbye.

They weren't thinking.

A stroll around SoHo would have been a nice idea, she thought.

A napoleon at Caffe Reggio, before hopping uptown, why not? He didn't really need to go to the office.

*I wasn't thinking.*

I wasn't either, she'd have replied.

# Tuesday

They hadn't discussed at what time they were to meet the next morning. So as not to miss each other, they both arrived an hour early, dressed very lightly this time: she was wearing a T-shirt with a linen scarf and wide, yellow linen trousers; he khakis, a light-blue button-down shirt, and a pair of loafers. His jade-green socks didn't bunch, she noticed.

Meeting fifteen minutes before jury selection would have meant arriving at the main hall just in the nick of time, especially following the crowd lining up before the metal detectors and then massing up by the elevators. Half an hour early might have meant waiting in line at the coffee place. An hour early meant finding a table, eating a leisurely croissant each, and ordering, who knows, a second espresso to drink on the way to the courts.

That they both arrived too early at Da Pirro told them what they were reluctant to admit to themselves while getting dressed that morning.

"If they impanel me, I might not be allowed to lunch. We'll have to arrange for coffee afterward."

"What if they sequester you?"

"We'll cross that bridge . . ." She didn't finish.

"Or jump off it."

Both knew instinctively that yesterday's humor had come back, and they relished how it settled between them with the coffee and croissants. Without explaining why, she took out her phone and they exchanged numbers. It was a spontaneous gesture, and the two of them were sufficiently canny not to read too much into it.

"I don't want to sound gloomy again, but it feels as if our time is being squeezed through an eyedropper."

He agreed. It was good to know that the other felt no differently.

He thought they'd text each other as things developed.

Yes, as things developed, she said with a touch of humor.

They laughed, the two of them realizing that, without meaning to, they probably sounded like a pair of old-school safecrackers synchronizing watches before blowing up the wall to the bank vault.

During their quick coffee and croissant before court, she wanted to know about his children. She had meant to ask him about his wife. Was he perhaps a grandfather?

Two sons, three grandchildren. He enjoyed devoting more time these days to tennis, chamber music concerts, books, classes at the gym, and art films. He had a house at the beach in East Hampton, but no one really went there. His sons had loved it years before, but now they shared a farm near Woodstock where they lived year-round. "They're very close. As for us, we're city dwellers now," he said. "And you?"

She had many patients and, like everyone in her profession, couldn't wait for August. She had a daughter, one grandson, a husband, no house at the beach, no house in the country. They preferred their monthlong travels around the world, with added shorter trips around Christmas and spring. Her husband was a shrink too, so August entailed serious traveling and all the planning that went with it—his project, not hers, she added with a note of sarcasm. She was too scatterbrained to plan as simple a thing as a trip abroad. This year he hadn't planned anything yet, she didn't know what was up with him. Last year they'd gone to Morocco, the year before to Guam, this spring to Tuscany, though they'd been there more times than she could remember. Same cities, same rentals, same walks, always a new ancient little town perched on a tiny Tuscan hill with its vintner and its artisanal, unpasteurized cheeses, its own famous portrait of the Virgin under a rotting church ceiling that needed restoring but that no town could afford to do a thing about. Grows tiresome after a while, she said. They weren't traveling this August. They used to rent a house in Rhinebeck, and like everyone, she missed the ordinary pleasures of Porta Yardia and Deck Island.

He laughed at the names.

"It's a tired old joke, but it holds up if you've never heard it before," she said, already smiling while using the very words he'd used the day before. He liked how she borrowed them and gave them back to him with a hint of a spin. He liked her unabashed candor and her quick flashes of humor. "You have beautiful eyes," he told her while they were still eating. People used to say that, she said, but when she tried to see for herself in the mirror, she couldn't tell what they were talking about. "It's like trying to catch your eyes rolling when you stare in the mirror. Impossible! Maybe knowing who we are is an equally impossible task, don't you think? We're constantly looking away."

"Take the compliment."

She smiled. "Trust me, I did."

He liked how she'd bandied this about too.

As for the rest of her, she added, it was all maintenance. Pilates, spin classes, yoga, the usual.

He asked to tear off a piece of her croissant after finishing his. She said she'd already had breakfast that morning. What did she normally eat? "Hemp seeds, flax, sunflower or pumpkin seeds, rolled oats, pistachios, golden raisins, and slivered almonds."

"Oh, we used to call it gorp. Ever get tired of it?"

"Totally. But it's super healthy. Sometimes I'll sneak a bowl of my grandson's Honey Nut Cheerios and eat them standing up in the kitchen."

"And the cilantro situation?" he suddenly asked, trying to steer the conversation to her husband and make her say more about him.

"The cilantro situation," she mused, thinking how to answer. Then, avoiding a reply, she simply added, "Not much different from yours, I presume."

He snickered, she did too. Ducking the delicate matter said much more than an elaborate answer.

"Difficult?" he asked, still trying to coax her to say something about her husband.

"As in the famous joke," she replied, still deflecting the matter without really doing so, "we own two old dogs. It would kill them."

"No dogs here, but same," he added.

"Are we speaking in code again?"

"How coded could we be if we both know what we're talking about?"

"*Right!*" she said, emphasizing the word. "Open codes. Almost like whispering in a movie theater when you're a teenager. You don't really hear what he's saying, but you have a good idea what he wants."

It made him laugh.

"I hope they won't select us and will let us go free soon," she added, changing the subject.

"Actually, I wouldn't mind this for another day or two. As long as they don't impanel us, this has all the makings of an impromptu mountain-lake vacation in the middle of scalding Manhattan."

"I agree," she said. "I'm enjoying this. Another few days like yesterday and today could be quite . . ." She couldn't decide which adjective sounded safe enough, so she let her sentence trail.

He had a vague sense of why she hadn't spelled out her meaning but could also tell that she didn't mind whichever meaning he inferred.

"So, tell me something else about yourself," she said.

"Is this the shrink asking?"

"In part, but not entirely. Did you really have mixed feelings about your work?"

"Not always. But it had its very dull moments. I wasted far too many years, and though I was good at what I did and the money and perks certainly didn't hurt, it left me no time to do what I had always wanted to do since my undergraduate days."

She gave him an inquisitive look.

"I wanted to study history. Now I read history and am still interested in the great historians of the ancient world and have reread almost all of them. But am I happy? I don't know. What's next? I don't know that either. Is there another chapter after retirement? I'm waiting to hear." He paused. "Have I given you more than you asked to know?"

"Not at all. Actually, what is it that you're still not telling me?" the shrink asked.

"Maybe what keeps me alive at this point is waiting for something unforeseen to come along. Call it retirement-plus. Good or bad doesn't matter, so long as it's a new leaf. My dream: to go to Greece and Italy, but mostly to visit the sites mentioned by Thucydides and Livy. I want to see Lake Trasimene for myself and understand how so many Romans could have perished so needlessly at the hand of the Carthaginians, or go to Plataea, which withstood Sparta for a while but whose women were finally sold into slavery and the men put to death after none could answer what he had done to serve the cause of Sparta in its long war against Athens. And I want to go to Syracuse, to see the spot where the Athenian general Nicias was put to death. These things don't go away because they happened more than two thousand years ago. Nothing goes away, including, as I'm starting to find out, the things we wished had happened but never did. Those rankle and stew in our hearts just the same, and if I were a shrink, I'd say they continue to goad us even when we're sure we've all but put them behind. But then that's your profession, not mine. Don't you want to go to Vienna or London, where Freud saw his patients?"

"I've been, but wouldn't mind going again. It's like therapy. Something new always drifts into the open when you see Freud's couch, Freud's desk, his collection of tchotchkes."

"I've never been to his home in London."

"I would love to show you around. It's fascinating. Jon hates house museums."

"And I'll show you the spot where Archimedes was killed. I've never shown it to anyone."

"I'd love to see that." Then, catching herself: "In another lifetime."

"Yes, that other lifetime," he mused. "Did you always want to become a psychologist?"

"No, I was a studio art major. I wanted to paint. But I had started to see a therapist as an undergraduate— bad boyfriend, invasive parents, no real friends—and I ended up having more insights into my shrink than he had into me. In fact, he encouraged me to change majors and study psychology. Then we dated for a while—he turned out to be far worse than the boyfriend I'd gone to see him about. So I dropped him and went back to my solitary life, which wasn't so bad and lasted a few years before I met Jon. The rest . . ."

"Tell me about your work."

"I like what I do. I like guiding my patients, prodding, and helping them to say what they mean to say despite the hurdles they've placed before themselves. I try never to guess what these hurdles are; I just know they're there and sometimes I'm taken aback by my sleuthing instincts, and this suspense-surprise makes me love my job sometimes. Still . . ."

But she didn't finish her thought.

"Still?"

"What did you call it? Retirement-plus versus retirement-lite. I need to decide."

He'd never been to see a shrink. "Why?" she asked.

"Either because I never quarreled with who I was or

because I was afraid of what I'd uncover and end up quarreling with everything."

"Well, there we are: the wannabe painter and the would-be historian."

They spoke about television series they enjoyed watching. Books they enjoyed rereading. Dinners with friends.

"So, are you happy?" he asked.

"Not unhappy. You?"

"Not unhappy either."

But then they laughed, realizing that they'd both applied the same glossy patina over their lives. What if, she thought, she'd taken down a layer of sheen for him? It reminded her of how she'd remove her makeup every night in front of her mirror, clear the foundation, clean her pores, and wash her face one last time before staring at what she really looked like, before applying her night cream and a special ointment around the bags under her eyes. Jon hated the taste of her night cream on the rare occasions when he attempted to make love to her. And maybe that's why she used the cream. One way or another, he'd say, there was always a layer of something between them. They frequently quarreled before sex, so sex wouldn't happen. Did he want her to look old before her time? she'd ask. No, not old, but unctionless, he'd say. Unctionless—whoever used such a word with his wife? Sometimes one of them took to the sofa. Then the years happened.

*Not unhappy*, she had said.

He was no better. He had nothing to complain about, really. He loved life with his wife, loved her view on so many things, always heeded her advice, even when he wasn't sure he agreed. He was an exemplary partner, never the litigious sort. He cooked dinner most nights of the week, did homework with the boys when they were young, read to them, edited their work when they'd email their college papers to him late Sunday afternoons, telling him they needed his edits by Monday morning at the latest, meaning by Sunday evening. When they were young he'd helped them build a tiny playpen for two hamsters. Everyone else's playpens broke the moment a hamster was released into them, but not his. The secret was wooden matches from a restaurant to reinforce each of the tiny fences built around the pen. His wife heard the tale and called it luck. It would have been luck, but it took something like engineering savvy, wouldn't she say? She wouldn't say, just walked out of the room, leaving father and sons gaping at each other with the sort of silent, mischievous complicity that would eventually wear out and disappear once they'd grown and moved away.

*Not unhappy either*, were his words.

This might have ended their little conversation over their improvised breakfast.

"We still haven't explained cilantro," she finally said.

He looked at her and simply said, "Thank you," because he was grateful that she had spotted all of his cunning little twists. "Who'll go first?" he asked.

"Actually, we don't need to. We already know, plus we have other plans. Chinese food for lunch. I want us to have exactly the same dishes, in the exact same place at the exact same time. I want nothing disturbed or changed. The least change may topple everything and send us into retroflex."

"Let's meet at twelve thirty-five downstairs in the lobby."

"We don't even need to synchronize our watches," she said. "If there's trouble, text me."

"As things develop," he quoted himself, an ironic glint on his features.

"Yes, we're good to go." Another cliché to go along with his.

Their lingo made them laugh again and feel uplifted.

At twelve thirty-five, however, they did not meet downstairs as planned. Instead, they met on the same elevator headed to the lobby. They weren't even able to conceal their excitement, nor did they attempt to. "This saves us three minutes," he said.

Did she really not want to try another place?

"Not really," she replied.

Same was perfect. The soup came immediately. Seven minutes for the soup, he said. Another seven for three dumplings each, and don't you dare touch any of mine, she said. If everything went according to plan, they'd even have time for an espresso at Da Pirro. "Why soup on such a sweltering day?" she asked. "Ritual," he explained, sensing that his mind and hers ran on parallel lanes and that this one word would cement their tacit understanding of what, with others, would have required a long, tiresome explanation. "Ritual," she repeated, confirming that indeed they thought along identical paths and didn't need a thing more said. And knowing this made them both very happy.

"What did you think?" she asked as soon as they walked out of the restaurant into the sweltering noon heat.

"Just perfect. Sated and satisfied," he replied. "One more day like this and our lives will be changed, we'll become better people, deal kindly with rivals, show tolerance to those we can't stand, and maybe discover the better things of life before it's too late."

"Well spoken. Sated and satisfied." She repeated his

words without telling him that these two words meant the same thing. "That's exactly how I feel."

"Coffee will be great."

They entered the same place where they'd had breakfast that morning.

"Are you part of the jury pool?" asked the young barista. He explained that people who return all the time—and this was their third time within twenty-four hours—are usually potential jurors who look hopelessly adrift.

Yes, they were.

"If I were to be tried for murder, I am sure I'd want you for jurors."

"Why?"

"You look very happy and are clearly not about to send someone to the gallows."

"We have seven minutes before we leave."

"I know, I'm working as fast I can," replied the barista. His sailor's beard and Italian accent made her ask where in Italy he was from.

"Naples," he replied.

"Naples," she sighed.

"I know," he said, looking all glum suddenly because it required no genius to interpret her sigh.

When was he there last? she asked.

"Three years ago. My mother, she passed away. And you?"

"Two Easters ago."

"Yes, Naples!" It was the barista's turn to sigh. "If my life were different, I'd head to the airport now and hop on the first plane to Fiumicino, then take a train from Termini to Piazza Garibaldi, and I'm home—Posillipo, Sorrento, Marechiaro, that's my paradise!"

"Who wouldn't want to be in Naples?" said Paul. "My mother was born in Naples. She never returned, though she always promised she would. She taught me one or two Neapolitan songs. I can sing a few bars, but I have no idea what I'm singing."

They tipped the barista generously. Then they left, arrived at the courthouse on time, and were made to sit in the large central room, where the jury warden gave his multiple apologies for the air-conditioning that was, he said, still on the blink and might decide to remain that way for the rest of the summer. He sympathized with them. Someone shouted, "Then let us go home!"

"If only," replied the jury warden.

"If by three o'clock . . . ," Catherine began loudly.

"By three o'clock you will go home. It's a promise."

By three they were indeed set free. "Subway?" he asked.

He caught the look she gave.

"I asked because I assumed you had pressing things to attend to once you got home."

"No, I'm in no rush."

"A napoleon at Caffe Reggio? I know you're big on healthy grains, but you'll enjoy it and we'll order two cappuccinos, and maybe, maybe, manage to pretend we're in Naples."

"My God, what a terrific idea. Do you always come up with such wonderful ideas? Chinese restaurants, Pirro's coffee, napoleons, cappuccinos, and let's not forget croissants in the morning—and now the whole thing topped off with an illusion of Italy."

"Strange you should say this. I seldom suggest anything, I always let my wife decide."

"How come?"

"We're entering the shuddering cilantro bush."

"Oh, just answer."

"She always comes up with better ideas."

"Or maybe because you don't want to risk suggesting the wrong ones. Happens in most couples. You must have done something very wrong with her long ago and were chastened and never wanted to be chastened again."

"Maybe. But I have no idea what I did, or what I've been afraid of. Besides, in your line it's always the patient's fault, isn't it?"

And with that, he hailed a cab and told the driver to take them up Sixth Avenue to Minetta Lane. She noticed the harsh, lapidary tone in the way he spoke to the cabbie—lawyerly, she thought—but she didn't want to let that faze her. She had never heard of Minetta Lane and was wondering where it could be.

An awkward silence hovered between them. She didn't like it and wanted it dispelled, just as she wanted their stuffy old courthouse hurled from their open window. She didn't like the hot air outside and in the car either. Clearly, she thought, the cabbie didn't want to turn on the AC. She wasn't going to say anything. Paul wasn't saying anything either.

To break the silent spell between them, all she could think of was to hold out her hand to him.

"My name is Catherine, and how do you do?"

She said it with a humorous lilt to her voice in imitation of British parlance. He wanted to laugh at first but stared at her in silence, not knowing what kind of game this was. "Your turn," she said with a playful, insistent note in her voice, as though she were running out of patience with him.

"Oh, and mine is Paul."

"Good," she said. "Now we know."

This time the two burst out laughing. It was her way of celebrating their budding friendship and allowing it to acquire a warmer cast than what they'd known in the jury hall.

"And how do you know Minetta Lane?" Catherine asked.

"Been going there for years. As a late teenager it's where I was stood up once and, to be honest, I never got over it and most likely made several girls pay for it."

"Including your wife?"

"Maybe even my wife."

"Which may explain why she put you in the doghouse that one time long ago. Maybe you felt you deserved being stood up at Caffe Reggio, just as you may find something uncannily familiar that takes you back to your origins each time you're blamed, or chided, or criticized. Maybe rebuke is your way of identifying an intimate and meaningful undercurrent in the story of your life, a blemish that nothing seems to wash off because, as we say in my line, *you haven't worked it through*."

He stared at her and could only exclaim: "Wow, Catherine, bull's-eye!"

"That was scratching the surface. On the house. All people have a weeping, hurt little child in them. Successful lawyers too. I've known a few."

"The funny thing is that, when you read the story of my life, the one thing that strings it all together is the list of what the French call my numberless *rendez-vous manqués*, my missed appointments, missed opportunities, missed encounters, big mistakes, and all those moments that almost happened but never did and still linger and won't ever give up long after I have. Caffe Reggio is a case in point."

The taxi zipped uptown and stopped at the entrance to Minetta Lane.

"I think we are in Italy this afternoon," Catherine said as soon as they sat down in the dark baroque room, which brought to mind those old, semi-gloomy places in southern Italy where the scent of baked pastries and ground coffee sweetens the air while the early-afternoon sun pounds the emptied pavements outside.

"I like this place," she said.

"You do, really?"

"Yes. Why do you sound so surprised?"

He could tell she had already guessed.

"So where were you seated when you were stood up?" Catherine asked.

He had meant to laugh but simply smiled. "Right where we're sitting now."

"Am I going to pay for it as well, then?" she asked.

He didn't know what to say and simply shook his head.

"You blushed, Paul."

"I know."

She looked at him. "It's sweet."

Their cappuccinos arrived in Caffe Reggio's signature orange-and-white porcelain cups and saucers. Then came the dessert de résistance, as she called it as soon as she saw its size. She took her fork and with it divided the napoleon in two equal parts, adding that she hadn't had *one of these* in eons. "Besides," she said, "it's been ages since I sat down for coffee and dessert with anyone who wasn't connected in one way or another to my work.

Maybe with my daughter, or my mother before she had dementia, or, to be honest, since graduate school." She thought about that for a moment.

"My mentor in graduate school once said to me that most patients don't want to change. What they want is to go back to who they thought they were before a crisis, before they lost their footing and felt that their lives had taken a wrong turn and been set adrift. Perhaps this is true of me as well. There are times when I wish to go back to who I once was."

"Before graduate school? Before your daughter?"

"Maybe."

"Or is it before cilantro?"

She did not answer. She could tell he understood why she didn't reply and was grateful he didn't press.

"But maybe your mentor was wrong," Paul said. "I don't think that people want to revert to who they were or to a time when things seemed better. What they want is something else, a new me that's been trailing them like a shadow but that they wouldn't recognize if it rang their bell or punched them on the nose. What we want, perhaps, is to borrow huge amounts from the life we know we're owed and then die before we're asked to pay any of it back. To die in hock."

"That kind of outlook would put me in hock and drive me out of business and force me into retirement-minus," she said. "What you may want is not a new you but simply to escape the you who got stood up and hasn't budged since and still wishes to rehabilitate himself."

"Bull's-eye again, doc!"

"Courtesy of my mentor and thesis adviser. Going back and forging ahead are ultimately one and the same thing—snakes and ladders, ghosts and shadows."

"I need to think this through."

His sudden silence made her smile, which made him smile as well. He loved new ideas, especially coming from someone who stares at you so candidly while watching you process what she just said.

"Or how about asking life for very little, Catherine. Jury duty, cappuccino, lunch in a rinky-dink hole-in-the-wall in Chinatown and half a napoleon, since this is what I've been reduced to eating this afternoon."

"I'm sorry, were you planning to gorge on the whole thing?"

"No, I loved how you did that with your fork."

He picked up his own fork and mimicked her gesture. He had liked her determined, graceful poise when splitting the napoleon in two. There was purpose in that gesture. But then he realized that what had moved him when she used her fork to split the napoleon was more than grace or purpose. There was kindness and caring and selfless goodwill that extended beyond her and reached out over to him as if she had meant to touch his hand but then decided not to. The word that came to him later that night when he kept going over her gesture at Caffe Reggio was *tenderness*. He remembered the way she had shaken his hand. There was humor and amity there as well. He had wanted to hold her hand too at that moment but had checked himself, thinking that a better moment was bound to occur again, though he felt it wouldn't, and indeed it hadn't.

They sipped their cappuccinos and looked around the emptied scene on MacDougal Street. It was very hot, and the asphalt, quietly shimmering under the afternoon sun, must have softened under the heat. What Paul missed on such glorious midafternoons, he said, was the presence of the sea. Just nearby, or even on one of those cheap frescoes you find in so many pizzerias around the world. She countered by reminding him he should take what life put on the table and not quibble about what was lacking. But then she changed her mind and said that he was right; a sea nearby would have added quite a bit. Walking along the shore . . . She did not finish her thought. They saw that other than the silent couple sitting outside on the café's sidewalk wearing hats and loosened shirts, the place inside was totally empty except for the man behind the counter ready to prepare drinks whenever an order came through and the young waitress standing and smoking absentmindedly in the doorway.

"I could use a cigarette now," he said.

She smiled. "I could too."

Both, it turned out, had quit smoking many years before.

"Do you miss it?" she asked.

"No. Do you?"

"No. But smoking did add something, though I'll never know what exactly."

"Maybe," Paul said, "it added a sort of aura on the fringe of things, like a surrogate life, the one we step into and never stay in long enough to know what it's like living there. So we smoke another cigarette and watch it burn out, and we're back each time standing outside on the sidewalk of our better lives, like exiting a movie theater from the side door on a Sunday evening and landing in an alleyway filled with piled-up garbage waiting for the Monday morning pickup. I liked who I was when I used to smoke. I knew it was bad for me, but I was fooled enough to believe that cigarettes led me back into my true Technicolor life. Like asking the usher standing by the exit door to let me back in again, and wanting the lights dimmed again, and the film started again, and to be given another go again. Do you think there is such a thing as a better life?"

"I'm a shrink, I have to believe. Sometimes striving is all we have. And frankly"—she half giggled self-consciously—"it's what keeps people like me in the profession."

They both felt their conversation was starting to drift. He changed the subject. "Are you a walker?"

"I'm wearing sneakers, aren't I?"

"What we can do to digest this napoleon, which was too sweet and too creamy, is walk to see a few galleries, if that is something you'd enjoy."

"For a man who never comes up with any ideas, you're exploding with them."

"The new me," he joked.

"Maybe the one trapped inside a pack of cigarettes trying to get out. Which kind did you smoke?"

"Kent. You?"

"Funny, funny, Kent also," she said.

"Do you think this could mean something?"

"Just a coincidence."

"Maybe I don't want it to be a coincidence."

"You mean because Freud didn't believe in coincidences?"

"No, that's not the reason."

He thought he understood what he'd just said, but wasn't sure he wanted to probe further. So he asked if she knew the one about the shrink and the shyster walking into a bar.

"No, I don't." She was already giggling.

"Each boasted how vital was his service to humanity. I protect people's spirit, said the shrink, and I protect their rights, countered the lawyer. Yes, but I can turn the soul around, snarked the shrink, and I can twist the law whichever way I please, spat the lawyer. In the end, the barman, who'd grown tired of their grandstanding, reminded them of one filthy trait they both shared. And what's that? they asked. You both get paid to hear people lie to you, he replied."

"Did you just make that up?"

"Yup. I think what you and I do is traffic in lies. We trade in shadowlands, where half-truths and lies by omission make good bedfellows. People think they're telling us the truth; they're not. They claim they want the truth; they don't. There comes a point when we no longer know what truth is, or worse yet, whether truth even matters. We speculate and we interpret, but that's not the truth."

"You may be right, but I'd never admit this to others."

"Would you tell this to your shaman shrink-meister?"

"Not in my life! Never!"

They finished their cappuccinos, paid, and tipped the waitress. He couldn't resist and told the waitress that she reminded him of the theater usher in Edward Hopper's painting.

She knew the painting and was thrilled by the comparison. What had made him think that?

The way she stood by the door, he said, pensive, almost absent, probably thinking of her boyfriend. She smiled and simply said, "Not boyfriend, girlfriend."

"I am so hopelessly old-school," he apologized.

She shook her head slightly to mean she didn't mind, it didn't matter, no offense taken—the kind of pardon one extends to a doddering grandparent who won't be around much longer and wouldn't understand anyway.

"Just like youth: stabs you first, and then twists the blade."

They hastened their pace, crossed Sixth Avenue, and walked farther west. On the short block of Carmine Street before they arrived at Bleecker Street, she told him a famous painting by John Sloan had captured the Sixth Avenue El exactly there. "Apparently when the El was taken down, no one wanted the scrap metal except—so legend has it—Japan, which imported the steel and with it built the planes that would eventually bomb Pearl Harbor."

How did she know that?

She'd read it somewhere.

When they reached Abingdon Square, it was his turn to say that, a few years earlier, he had fallen head over heels for a woman who made him feel older than her father by at least a decade.

"Stabbed and twisted?" she asked with a wry smile on her face.

"I took it well," he said, "which is to say I'll probably never recover."

"How many times have you never recovered?"

He saw the joke.

"If I go back to kindergarten, hundreds. Does one truly ever recover?"

"I should know, right? I don't think we ever do recover. We're just layered with traumas and heartbreaks, some very deep, others on the surface, and before you know it, the ones on the surface sink to the very bottom and seem to go away, while those all the way below rise up again, as in a lava lamp. In fact"—and she thought for a while before continuing—"I used to own a lava lamp, and it was the inspiration for my dissertation:

every time I forgot what I was writing about, all I had to do was stare at my lava lamp, and there, winking at me, was my subject. We are, all of us, little lava lamps, wobbling about trying to figure who we really are, what we want, where we're headed." Again she stopped and gave herself a moment. "You know, I haven't spoken like this in ages."

She paused again.

"Even with your husband, who is in the same profession?" Paul asked.

"I should say especially with my husband. In grad school we used to discuss these kinds of things to no end—so much to say, to learn. Maybe that's even why we got married. He was ahead of me by three years, so I always deferred to him, and soon he grew used to this and never changed. Now, occasionally, I disagree with him when he's wrong, and it surprises him, disappoints him, so I shrink back into a form of strained docility to keep the peace. Ironically, it is familiarity that estranges people. We repeat the same things till we run out of new ways to say them, then we grow tired of saying them and of hearing them said, and our guarded silence turns into a way of life until we find ourselves drifting like two rudderless steamboats with their engines off. We mistake familiarity for intimacy. It is not intimacy. All it is, is habit—and habit is a shorthand for silence.

"We talk so very little," Catherine went on, "as if silence hasn't just become a way of life but our way of holding off saying the two to three words that could undo everything. Silence is our nickname for muffled hostility. For a conversation to unroll between two persons you need a base of sympathy. People with completely different ideas and incompatible interests, if they share a degree of sympathy and warmth between them, can talk for hours. People with identical interests, without sympathy, live in silence. Plus, he's curt and abrupt with me. And I understand why. So to compensate and keep our barge floating, I put myself down a bit, but then he uses my alleged insecurities to demean me even more, which explains why he finds fault with the monthly bills I send my patients, or why he claims I've yet to learn how to speak to my grandson, and just last night he joked about my being a juror. I let him. You see, sometimes habit needs new filters, even obstacles, the way old houses need new hedges and new trees. With strangers, intimacy happens so suddenly, precisely because we're less on our guard and there are no habits yet. I can think of two in particular."

"You mean the two who met in the central jury room and had lunch in a Chinese restaurant and can't stop talking and are beginning to open up too much—"

"—and are scared that all this may just die post–jury duty?"

"You think it might—die, that is?" Paul asked.

"I hope not, but who knows."

"Are you happy we've met?"

"Yes, I am. Very. You?"

"Very much."

And without planning it, he raised his palm and touched her cheek.

She didn't seem to mind. But, looking him straight in the face, she asked, "Were you flirting with me just now?"

"I thought I was confiding."

"Yes, confiding, but borderline something else too."

"And that's so terrible, isn't it?" he said with sarcasm lilting in his voice.

"I don't know. The jury isn't impaneled yet. Have you really read *Wuthering Heights* twice?" She wanted him to know she too knew how to change the subject abruptly.

"Actually, I read it more than twice, but then you would have thought me a true kook, the kind who stares at you in a subway car, tries to make conversation if he so much as catches a glint in your eye, and then button-holes you for life."

When the two reached one of the art galleries, they saw that it was exhibiting abstract art, which they stared at with a degree of curiosity that could never pass for delight. They walked out of the gallery without saying goodbye.

In the gallery next door, they saw a small painting they truly loved. They toured the gallery, then returned to the same painting, looked at other works by the same artist, and for the third time came back to it. It was a picture of a seascape from a balcony in Nice or Collioure or somewhere else on the Mediterranean, and most likely from a hotel room. And while they were both staring at it, he said, "I could just live in that room overlooking the sea."

What a thing to say, she thought, suddenly realizing for the first time: this man isn't happy. "Maybe it's the view from your famed Hotel Segreto."

"Could be, could just be." He would never have thought of that, but she was right.

The young lady at the gallery could see that they liked the painting and explained who the painter was, where he'd painted it, and where it belonged in the larger collection of his work. He had lived in San Sebastián and Antibes, then moved to southern Italy, she said. Could they take a picture of it with their iPhones? Yes, of course, said the owner of the gallery, who, sensing a possible sale, had come over to rescue her assistant, who was clearly a novice.

Paul took a picture of the painting. So did Catherine.

Would either of them buy it? they wondered once they were outside and kept staring at their iPhone photos. "I'd love to, certainly on impulse, but the problem is, where would I hang it?" Paul asked.

"Perhaps in your secret hotel room in Naples," she teased.

He got the hint but did not respond. What he liked most was how well she read every sinuous bend in his character, and not just because she was a shrink, but because she bored into him and felt the pulse of his thoughts, his feelings, his hopes, his desires, down to his faults, and of course his regrets. It thrilled him—either because it happened so very, very seldom in his life, or simply because it came from her. If she spotted blemishes, he didn't mind. He liked it.

They entered a third gallery, roamed about the space, pretended to admire the installations, but then, on seeing that this was the last gallery on that particular stretch, decided to turn back to revisit their favorite small painting. It was more stunning the second time. It had acquired a certain familiarity, as though it already belonged to them and had been removed from their wall and, by sheer happenstance, ended up in this tiny gallery in Chelsea. If it belonged to them, he thought, then surely they were already living together.

"What would Mr. Cilantro say?" he finally asked as they were walking toward the entrance to the High Line.

"Cilantro would frown, learn to tolerate it, pretend to love it, but there'd always be that residual shadow of contempt. And Mrs. Cilantro?"

"Claire," he said. "She'd be neither hot nor cold, and there'd be resistance too, but she'd grow to love this painting."

"We should buy it, and, unlike Solomon's baby, slice it in half, and each hang our half in our private space in our shadow home," said Catherine.

*So we have a home?* he was going to ask. Instead: "So you have a shadow home?"

"Doesn't everybody?"

"I suppose."

"People seldom admit to having one, but for a few seconds each and every day, without even knowing it, they'll slip into their unlived lives, some while showering alone, where they'll talk to themselves, sing to themselves, or even dance to music emanating from some other room. Some cry in the shower, hoping no one hears, others laugh out loud at incidents they still find funny but are wise enough to keep bottled up in company."

"So," he said, "some of us smoke cigarettes to squirrel into our imaginary cubicle for a few minutes, while others just stand and wash."

"Exactly. Others—and don't ever quote me—pay me by the hour to be alone with themselves."

"You make what you do sound trivial."

"Trust me, there are people who believe mine is no different from the oldest profession."

They laughed.

"Well, years ago this area at night would have been

the right neighborhood for the oldest profession," Paul said. Then, stepping on the stairs to the High Line, he turned around and said they should stroll.

The place was teeming with tourists speaking in every tongue imaginable. Babel. Close by, they watched a busker playing a tenor saxophone, then, leaving the bottlenecked passage along one of the overgrown paths, stopped not far from an old man who was sitting on a bench staring absently at Hoboken station across the Hudson, looking lost and forlorn.

"I wonder what his day has been like," she said.

"Not happy. And what's sadder yet is that he's probably thinking that the rest of it won't be any better."

Unable to resist the impulse, she approached the man and sat at the edge of the bench next to him and asked what kind of thoughts he was nursing.

"Not happy thoughts," he replied, perfectly poised and well-spoken. She asked him why.

"My wife doesn't recognize me at all these days, doesn't even know who she is, and speaks to me in Croatian. I'm from Hungary, so we could only speak in English, but English began to lose its words for her, and now, like a ghost, English is gone out the window of her life, which means that everything we had is lost as well, which makes me a ghost too, and I don't want to be."

"Is she alone at home?"

"No, she has her nurse, then our son and grandsons will come later in the afternoon to keep her company."

"How long have the two of you been together?"

He looked up and smiled at her. "Since we met almost sixty years ago."

"Good years?" she asked.

"Yes, quite good," he replied, "but what does that

mean now? We can no longer speak. Everything's been erased. And I'm so tired of her condition. I'm tired of the nurses, tired of my son and of our grandchildren, tired of everyone. I want to be alone. So I come here."

"And here I am bothering you." She apologized.

"No apology needed, please. But thank you for speaking to me. It's so rare to speak with a stranger who understands."

"I'm a psychologist. If I didn't understand, who would?"

"Strange," he said, staring at her for a few moments without saying another word. Then: "I was a psychiatrist once, but long ago. I should never have stopped. But I did."

The old gentleman stood up and the two shook hands, exchanging names. He did not return to his seat but walked away, and eventually they watched him leave the High Line.

"Sad," said Paul.

"Very."

"I suppose this is how it ends, unavoidably."

They both knew what that sentence meant, but neither wanted to discuss it or clarify its meaning.

They retraced their steps on the High Line and took the exit back to Twenty-Third Street, then descended the two flights of stairs. They dawdled about for a while, chitchatting, then realized as they started walking that what they were doing was heading to their respective subway stops. She was taking the uptown C on Eighth Avenue, he the uptown Lexington local. Probably, he'd make a short stop at Eataly to pick up some fresh greens, he said. But when they passed by London Terrace, she told him that she'd grown up there and had lived there long before meeting her husband. Her parents had moved to Florida and allowed her to take over their place while she attended NYU.

"I can't believe it," he said. He had lived there too. When they compared years, they discovered that he had lived there for only two of her years in the building, 1978 to '79. They asked each other how old they had been at the time, which they almost regretted asking, as this was an involuntary way of disclosing their ages.

"We might have met," she said.

"We most likely did. I was a rookie lawyer at the time and had just moved to New York after finishing law school."

To their greater amazement yet, they discovered that both had lived in the same building, No. 405. "We definitely met, then."

"I was a budding shrink, very, very post-hippie lefty, wore leotards all the time but had never danced. Everyone wore purple leotards in those years."

"And I was a stuck-up young lawyer, all attitude, always walking in and out of the office with my gym bag and squash racket."

"We might have met in the grocery store downstairs or at the cleaner's or the swimming pool or by the mailboxes. Or just in the elevator. We would easily have met in the elevator."

"What does this say?" he asked.

"Should it say something?" she asked, in that typically veiled shrink way that implied she was about to pry open long-held secrets.

"You know it does."

"You mean something about us back then?"

He hesitated a moment. "No," he said.

"Maybe it's a good thing we're separating here," she

said when they arrived at the Eighth Avenue station. There was no hint of admonition in her tone. Her words, he realized, were meant for herself as well.

"Tomorrow morning?" she asked.

"Absolutely."

## Wednesday

The next day they met even earlier. She was not wearing a scarf or makeup, just a light-turquoise jumpsuit and a different pair of sneakers, her upper arms and shoulders once again exposed. He was wearing a straw hat, a white button-down shirt, the same chinos, and was carrying a light canvas backpack. They could have been headed for the beach.

"We're not formal. It might bring us bad luck. We could be forcing fate's hand by assuming we won't be impaneled. I'm too superstitious for that," Catherine said.

"Despite being a shrink?"

"I believe in magical thinking, okay? Don't tell my patients. It's one of my vices."

"How many do you have?"

"One day! One day!" she repeated, meaning that one day, perhaps, she might tell him.

"I'll wait."

They sat, eager to speak during the short time they knew they had.

"This is so much fun," she said as soon as their two

croissants—or *cornetti*, as the barista called them—were brought to their table along with two double espressos.

Still, so much to say and so little time.

"Well?" Catherine finally asked, not knowing why she'd said it or what she meant by it.

Paul too was feeling the rise in tension. "Did you think of me last night?" he finally heard himself ask. His was an innocent question that simply meant to pick up where they'd left off the day before, but his "last night," thrown in before he had time to quash it, sounded unnecessarily bold, and he was more worried about making her feel uncomfortable than about revealing uncensored thoughts she'd easily make out. "I'm sorry, I think my question came out all wrong—would the jury strike it from the record?"

"I thought lawyers never asked questions without already knowing the answer."

"Maybe I was not being a lawyer. Maybe I was asking a simple person-to-person question."

She looked at him, then tore off the tapered end of her croissant. "What did you expect me to say?"

Since there was no backpedaling now: "I wanted you to say yes."

"Then yes."

The tone of her answer seemed intentionally evasive, even jolting, and did not satisfy him. "So let me ask differently: Did you think of me last night?"

"Of course I did. Why, didn't you think of me?"

"You mean last night?"

"Yes."

"I forgot to." He was trying to contain his laughter but couldn't. "A lot, actually." Then, as though on second thought: "I wished you were in my evening class at the gym, I wished we were going to have dinner, I wished so many things. Hasn't happened in ages."

"Are you flirting with me, again, Paul?"

"To be very honest, I don't know."

"Then you must be flirting."

"I suppose I am, then."

"One never knows with you."

"Honestly, I never know with myself either."

Neither knew who was joking and who was not, which is why she finally accused the two of them of behaving like clowns.

Seeing them both laughing so heartily, the barista interrupted and offered a free cornetto. He said he had made them himself. When he went back behind the counter, Paul said, "This place is another doorway to Italy. You, me, being here, starting early every morning. Feels like we've dropped everything and are waiting in the shade of a little Italian café before braving the heat on our way to take a tourist bus to Caserta, where I've never been—"

"So," she suddenly broke in, "have you told your wife why you slip out so early in the morning?"

"You mean have I told her about you? No. Have you?"

"Told my wife?" she joked. "No. Tell me about her. You never speak about her. What does she do—Claire, right?"

"She is a senior editor at a fashion magazine. Keeps her up many nights, travels a lot, loves it."

Back to the grandchildren. Did he see them often?

"Seldom. Their fathers work all the time and never come to the city. Whenever we went to visit them, they were too busy to spend more than half an hour with us.

So we stopped going. I Skype with the grandkids. But almost never. And you?" he asked.

"All the time," she said. Her grandson was the apple of her eye. Thoughts of him brought an expansive smile to her face. Paul smiled back, both to mirror her joy and to let down his guard and express, without saying it, that he too had a weakness for grandchildren.

Then they stood up and left Da Pirro. They crossed the street and resumed their seats in the main hall's waiting room.

Not five minutes later she was summoned on the PA. He wished her good luck.

"Good luck to you too," she said. "And don't disappear. Please. There's so much I want to know."

"Me too," Paul said. "Meet you right here."

By quarter past twelve it was clear that something was amiss. He'd been reading and was starting to feel restless. Either she'd been impaneled or she was let go and simply decided to head home. He recognized that tinge of anxiety when you begin to despair and are almost set to give up but continue to wait. He'd told her about this at Caffe Reggio. This, he thought, could easily end up at the bottom of the lava lamp, and if it ever bounced up, it might do so years from now. Or he'd forget her soon enough. Gabbing with a perfect stranger was not unwelcome, and things were getting a touch sticky, and maybe splitting now was for the best. She was probably thinking the very same thing. Besides, he could easily persuade himself that he hadn't really counted on seeing her again. *We had our moment*, he thought, remembering the very word he'd used the day before. She was someone who was better than no one, the way he too was someone better than no one. Still, a pity.

Just after one o'clock she did show up.

"The jerks!" She was breathless, either because she had raced to the room or was still agitated after her verbal tussle with the prosecutor.

"Tell me slowly," said Paul.

"The kid had just turned eighteen, was accused by the police of robbing a store, and frankly he radiated more innocence than the policeman, who looked like an overstuffed sausage filled with fat, venom, and racism. I said that I would be impartial if the policeman took a lie-detector test. Had he? No. But the kid had—yes? I asked. Why trust the police if he looked like a brute chewing gum in court? I thought to myself. I was summarily excused. But I gave the policeman and the prosecutor the dirtiest looks. I was outraged. And they call this a fair trial!"

"Did you want to be a juror in the case?"

"No."

"Then you acted like a hysterical person, and that frequently works. The bad news is that we'll have to skip lunch. There isn't time until they summon us back again," he said.

That morning she had bought M&M's. "Lunch," she said, brandishing the unopened brown pack. He had Tums in his backpack. "We'll have to be very, very inventive," he concluded.

"One red M&M for me, one blue for you."

"I don't like blue," he said.

"Okay, then you get two yellows and I still get my red."

"Why two yellows?"

"Because each yellow is worth half a blue. Everyone knows."

"I see."

Then they both realized that in all their years they had never counted how many M&M's were in an ordinary brown pack.

"Funny, no one ever counts these. One just gobbles them up," Catherine said.

"Does one win if one has three of one color plus a pair of others, as in a full house?"

"Yes, you do win, unless the other person has four of the same color. Everyone knows."

"I'd like a yellow one," he said. And, without looking inside the pack, which she was holding open for him, he proceeded to put his hand in.

"Raise or fold?" she asked.

They laughed when indeed he blindly managed to pick a yellow one.

"This is fun," said Paul.

"I know."

"I know one more thing," he said, looking straight at her.

She looked back at him to show she'd already guessed.

"Don't say it."

"But you do know."

"I think I do."

"Would I be crossing a line?"

She thought awhile. "You're putting me on the spot."

"I know."

Then, realizing that he might have overstepped: "Did I suggest anything that wasn't true?"

"I'm not going to answer that."

"Then you just did."

They ate the last M&M's.

A few moments of silence elapsed.

"I got scared there," he said.

"When?" she asked. Was he thinking of the M&M's, or was it something else? "What scared you?"

"I thought you weren't coming back."

"I would have texted you; I would have told you. Why scared?" she protested.

This moved him. *You know exactly why*, he would have said, but kept quiet. Meanwhile, the hall had gotten so hot that the jury warden got on the PA and told everyone to go home and be back the next morning, nine thirty sharp.

"Hungry?" he asked.

"Not really." She was no longer hungry.

He had just said it to be together a while longer, but he wasn't hungry either.

Catherine said she wanted an ice-cold bottle of sparkling water. He said he wanted one too. What buoyed his spirit was that they weren't separating so soon.

Back to Da Pirro, where they stood in line.

"No jury today?" asked their friendly barista from Naples.

"We were dismissed. Too hot," she explained. Then, as she ordered two bottles: "Which part of Naples do you like best?"

"Any part." And with this he started singing, with an amazing voice, words from an Italian song. "It's a song composed by a man born in Bologna, not Naples, but it's about Caruso, who returns to spend the last days of his life in a hotel in Naples."

A couple in the shop asked him to sing that refrain

again, and the barista, after demurring a few moments, was happy to oblige. But then, "The wish to cry comes," he said in his unidiomatic English. And indeed, after singing a few more bars, he removed his Ray-Ban sunglasses and, taking a paper napkin from the dispenser on the glass counter, began wiping his eyes.

"And where are you two going?" he asked, asking Catherine and Paul from his spot behind the counter.

"We don't know."

"I tell you what," he said, pointing at Paul, "you put on my apron, come behind the bar, and let me take the lady for a short walk."

It was not clear whether he was joking, but she responded in a way that surprised Paul.

"Not possible. He's with me, and I'm with him."

"In that case, *ce vedimmo mañana*," he said, mixing Neapolitan and Spanish. "Clearly, you don't love me."

Catherine reached over the counter and kissed him on the cheek.

"My name is Pirro."

"Mine, Catherine."

"And that was not flirting?" Paul said as they walked out with their bottles of cold water.

"Maybe. But I'm happy today."

Walking briskly, it took them less than half an hour to arrive at the foot of the High Line. The air was muggy and hot, but neither minded. The High Line was in full bloom and thronged with tourists.

"If I shut my eyes, within two seconds I could be in Italy," she said, almost picking up where she had left off the day before at Caffe Reggio.

"Me too. What do you like about Italy?" Paul asked.

"Everything. Summer, the cities, the towns, the faces,

the water, the people, their temper, their impatient yen to cut corners, their food, their wines, their old grand-mothers, their children, their intrusive kindness, even their shallow, unabashed temper when they're angry. They've never forgotten what it means to be human."

"Do you think we have?"

"The word from the people I see in my office tells me we've definitely lost something. I may have too."

He thought a moment and did not say anything. Then: "I have a terrific idea, but it's a mad idea. You and I should fly to Italy."

"Do you think we'd be able to stand each other after two days?"

"Maybe, or maybe not. I find my wife difficult when we're traveling."

"Oh, if that's where you're headed, I'm no longer sure that someone might find anything to like about me, much less to tolerate. Sometimes I feel I'm done with having someone else in my life. Or that I have nothing to offer. Or let's say I can no longer understand why people want each other, or what others are for. Maybe, like our old Hungarian friend, better to be completely alone than to feel alone with someone. Our imagined Italy could turn into such a disaster."

"If it's any consolation, by the time we're each back home tonight we'll have changed our minds and thought the whole trip totally senseless." He laughed at his own reading of his proposal.

She nodded, yes, it would indeed be senseless.

"Neither of us really wants to go abroad," she said. "As you yourself said, intimacy among strangers is fast and easy. Plus . . ."

"Plus?"

"We're just two ordinary, lonely people who happen to be married and at this point may not want the furniture moved around too much."

"Yes and no," he said. "We may be lonely, even ordinary, but we've been happier and more thrilled to meet than I've been in a very long time. It's been years since I've felt as welcomed to be who I am or feel as interesting as I have been these past few days. I've forgotten what it's like to be with someone who is eager to laugh with me, to know what I like, what I think, and with whom I'm dying to speak every day."

"Look," she said, and with that one word he could feel a chill note rise in her speech, "we are each in our own way enjoying this new wind in our lives, but we also know it can't infringe on our other life. I like you, Paul. We talk about serious things interspersed with pure gibberish. We like who we are together. I don't want this to end either, and if we have to have Chinese food for every lunch in the weeks and months to come, I would not say no. I hope our friendship has a life beyond jury duty. And let me be perfectly honest, there is no one else in my life. You have chamber music, art films, history books, your office, and God knows what else you haven't told me. I have my grandson, my daughter, my patients, and, for the past few days, you."

The sun was starting to glare at an oblique angle, blinding everyone staring at the Hudson. People were placing the flats of their palms over their eyes as they caught the Statue of Liberty in the distance. He wondered how those visiting New York would remember this moment. "For many, New York is the center of an imaginary universe—everywhere else feels peripheral, and stepping on its ground is the most miraculous, life-affirming moment, when they finally touch this holy grail of cities. When they go back to Arezzo or cold Rouen or rainy Brighton, they'll have this inscribed on their souls and it will radiate for years to come. We touched New York, they'll say. We were on the High Line and we saw this man and this woman walk upon the ancient parallel rails trying to keep their balance, though they couldn't bring themselves to hold hands."

She stopped walking. "Why did you say that?"

"Why? Fifteen, twenty years ago this would have been so simple, so obvious. Now I find myself dreading it might lead where neither of us wants it to go. So we're being very, very sensible. Am I wrong?"

She looked at him with a wistful and rueful glance that he'd never seen before, and he imagined this was how she stared at her patients when they'd finally dare to ask a bold personal question about her life. Did she honestly think he was wrong?

"No, I don't think you're wrong."

She could easily have said *Yes, you are wrong.* But she didn't.

"I don't know what it is," Paul said, "but I haven't felt anything in so long. And it's just nice to know I can still feel things. The restaurant in Chinatown, Pirro's place, the old man who said he just wanted to be alone, the napoleon you split in two the way you did, the gallery, getting all worked up when I think you've been impaneled or fearing you've been released and decided to go home and won't be showing up again—I keep repeating this list, which gets bigger and bigger because I never want to forget any of it. I like feeling this way. I get up in the morning and can't wait to have my first cup of coffee, not at home but with you, and I have this hunch that you leave home without your complicated breakfast to eat a small sugared croissant with me. And thinking this, even if I'm totally wrong, pins a halo, as you say, to my entire day."

A young couple walked between the two of them and came so close that the girl smiled and apologized.

"Russians," he said. "No, Poles."

Maybe it was watching the two lovers pass by and envying them, maybe it was the tenor that their conversation had taken, but he held her hand in both of his and, without giving the gesture any thought, brought it to his lips.

She did not pull her hand away, nor did she seem wary or surprised.

He was holding what he'd once thought was the hand of a pianist.

"Why?" she said a few moments later, obviously referring to his gesture.

"Just let me, please. I'm so grateful for these past three days, you have no idea. I could explain, but then I'd embarrass myself completely."

"Why?"

"If you ask it's because you wouldn't understand."

"Because I was born yesterday, right?" Catherine asked.

She looked at him. "Here," she said, and she suddenly hugged him, and in hugging him leaned her head on his shoulder.

Theirs were small, strained, self-conscious gestures, and, in the backs of their minds, they probably felt that they were just lucky enough to have found someone they could talk to and be themselves with, knowing that this could end in a matter of minutes.

"Better now?"

He simply nodded.

"You're different when I hold you," he said.

"I'm still me. You're different too," she said. "We could so easily revert to being good neighbors who've re-connected years after, riding the elevator in London Ter-race one evening. Which makes me wonder," Catherine added, with rising zest in her voice announcing a touch of humor as she finally released her hug, "did we sleep together back then?"

He smiled, pretended to be embarrassed. "Frankly, I can't remember."

It made them both burst out laughing.

"Let's sit down for a moment," she said, indicating a bench that had just been vacated by a group of tourists, a mother, a father, and a teenage daughter. They were too bewitched by Manhattan to think of the two who now sat down on their bench and were themselves totally en-grossed in their conversation. A moment of silence ensued.

He figured she wanted to reflect on things while watching people filing along the High Line. He decided to keep silent and not interfere. But she looked at him. "Talk to me, Paul," she said.

He shook his head very lightly, not to mean no, but to indicate rather that he simply lacked the words for what to say.

She shrugged her shoulders, meaning, *Say anything, really, I don't care.*

But seeing he was saying nothing, she was the one to speak.

"I live with silence, Paul, and I hate it. Silence is like looking at those around you from an open casket and wondering, why won't anyone talk to you?—you can hear them, so why can't they hear you? And then you realize that you don't want to talk either. This is why people die:

when there's nothing to say. No more talking. No more touching. No more hugging." She paused for a second. "Hold me, please," she said.

And he embraced her again and remembered what it was like to hug and want to hug someone.

"I like this," she said. "What kills me more than walking into our respective homes, like Cinderella rushing back to mop away the scent of our idyll on the High Line, is fearing how easily we could disappear from each other once we're back in our shabby little lives, like mirthless characters who stare blankly out the window and can't tell whether it's a person or the window they're desperately craving to hear from. In the weeks to come, it will be such a bother, or seem such a far-fetched trek, to even manage a cup of coffee across the park from each other that we'll just let it all slide. We're so sensible and so fainthearted, you and I."

"What do you think those tourists who left us our bench will say about us when they get back to wherever they came from?"

"They'll say they saw this couple in their mid-to-late sixties who still held each other after forty years together."

"Two would-be lovers trying to slip back into a past that never was."

"I fear tomorrow's jury selection. It's like playing Russian roulette and knowing we've cleared all the chambers except the last two. So now the odds are no longer in our favor. We have so little time."

"Catherine and Heathcliff had very little time too. What would they think?" he asked, trying to make light of what she'd just said.

"They had the afterlife and an indelible past. We

shrinks don't do the afterlife, and as for the past, we're still learning how to scratch its surface."

As time was inching toward six o'clock, they decided to leave the High Line. "Funny," she said. "Here we are imagining what these tourists will tell their families about New York, never thinking for a second that this man and this woman who held hands and hugged on the High Line share their exact same fantasy, but in reverse. Theirs is set in New York—they want to be Americans, eat American, speak American—whereas we can't wait to be Italians."

As they had done the previous afternoon, they got off at Twenty-Third Street and were going to walk past London Terrace again, but at the last moment, they turned the other way and headed to the art gallery. It made them laugh to realize that, without saying a word, they had acted on the same impulse.

They entered, were welcomed, and walked straight to the small painting they'd seen a day earlier. They loved the open French windows, loved the wrought-iron banister, and the view of the sea, and the color of the sea, and the faded orange armchair, loved it too.

"One day," Paul said, "maybe, we'll come together on a cold January morning to find that the painting was sold long ago, and, if we're lucky, we'll still be together, still rushing through our hasty lunch and trading pleasantries with that Italian barista, the two of us forever waiting to be impaneled in what's long become a shadow jury."

"Or," she added, "we'll return in the icy cold of winter and, on entering the gallery with fear in our hearts, spot the painting still there, unsold, still waiting, like the better part of our unlived lives."

## Thursday

"*Eccoli*, there they are," exclaimed Pirro the next morning. "I knew you'd be back."

They ordered two coffees and two cornetti.

"You mean the usual?" said the barista.

"Do you always remember?" Catherine asked.

"You, my dear, are special, and for you it's on the house."

She argued about that. She lost, of course, but just as they were walking out, she handed him a generous tip.

"Did he deserve it?" Paul asked.

"He made us feel young," she said. "It was all nonsense, but for a split second we believed him—and that little lie left a long footprint."

She turned red. "Shrinks don't blush," she said with humorous self-reproach.

They recalled their afternoon together. "We had a lovely time walking on the High Line again. I wonder what happened to the tired old man staring at the decaying turret of the Erie Lackawanna station across the river."

She did not respond. She seemed absent and taken by vague, faraway thoughts. "I liked that we talked about

Italy again," she said with an unforeseen, confiding tone. "I loved our little painting, and then we hugged and you kissed me at the subway stop."

"The last time I kissed someone that way outside the stairway of a subway station, I must have been, what, twelve, thirteen?"

"Did you think of me last night?" she asked, interrupting him.

"Just in passing. Did you?"

"Hardly at all."

They laughed.

"I couldn't wait to be alone to think of you," he said.

"Same. So, how old are we now?" she asked.

"Twelve, going on ten."

"Pretty soon we'll discover that what our parents did at night nine months before our birth was downright gross and disgusting."

That made him laugh. "Last night I thought of you and kept waking up every three minutes. You were staring at me and I was staring at you and we didn't say a word. Did I answer your question?"

She understood, she nodded. "I wanted to see you too. I feared it might never happen after today, and this didn't make me happy."

"Question before they call out our names and summon us to court again. But promise to answer honestly?" Paul asked.

"I can't guarantee that I will."

"Well answered. But," he said, staring at her, "when was the last time?"

"The last time what?" But as usual by now, she knew exactly what he was asking. "Honestly, I can't remember. You?"

"Can't remember either."

"Whose fault, yours or hers?"

"Mine, most likely. The truth is that neither one of us is able to recall what made us rush to intimacy once. Men usually complain it's the wife who stopped. But I know I'd been neglecting her for a while, and one day she made her peace with it, and never forgave me."

"And have you . . . slipped—with others, that is?"

"The last time was with the one who made me feel older than her father. Of course, I couldn't blame her," he added. "She was young, desirable, and could rouse a dead man's libido, but there was absolutely nothing to say when we were alone together. Lunch in a Chinese restaurant would have been murder, and as for walking the High Line, too boring for words. And you?"

"Years back, yes. Not a long story. Maybe I'll tell you about that indiscretion over lunch one day."

Then, changing the subject: had she brought M&M's in case the same mishap occurred?

She had completely forgotten.

"We'll have to ration our Tums, then. Tums on an empty stomach! Ugly business."

But they met for lunch as planned. It was so perfectly timed that, after leaving the restaurant, they took a leisurely walk.

"Da Pirro?"

"Absolutely."

When they entered, Pirro was busy with more customers than they'd ever seen before. "You made my day," he said to Catherine, and turning to Paul: "Are you sure you don't want to be a barista this afternoon? It's a wonderful life."

"Why, so you can steal her?"

"Of course."

"You Italians!"

They didn't have to order. He knew already what they wanted and, to top it all off, threw in four biscottini.

"And *niente mancia* today, no tip, *capito*?"

"*Capito*," she said.

"*E il bacio*, what about the kiss?" he asked, pointing to his cheek.

As she'd done the day before, she leaned over the glass counter and kissed him on both his bearded cheeks.

Someone took out his iPhone and wanted to take a picture, but it was too late. So Pirro asked the young man to get his iPhone ready this time.

"One more time," he told Catherine, who readily complied with another kiss.

"I think it makes him a bit jealous," she said, turning to look at Paul and smiling tenderly at him.

"Even better," said Pirro.

Paul welcomed her glance, and, probably to show the kiss hadn't fazed him, asked Pirro the name of the song he had sung the other day.

"Why you want to know?" came the question in his usual broken English.

"Because I will download it. Because we can't stop thinking of Naples."

He gave them the song's name.

"If we do go to Naples, what can we bring back for you?" she asked.

"What can you bring me—maybe a *panzerotto*."

"What is it?"

"It's a turnover, very much like a calzone, but smaller.

I'll be in heaven. Though to be honest, I make my own, which are more delicious here in New York than in Naples. But then, even my *panzerotti* feel homesick!"

The two eventually stood up and headed to the courthouse.

Minutes after they sat down in the large but no longer crowded central hall, they watched the jury warden seize the PA microphone and announce that they were all free to go home. They would be paid for their time, but shouldn't rush to leave before being given their certificate. "If ever you're summoned again before two years, the certificate will be your only proof that you served as a juror. We do not store a copy."

They started calling the names of those whose certificates were about to be handed out. Eventually, Catherine's name was announced over the PA. She was flustered and pleased and rushed to get her certificate as if it were a diploma. She returned to her seat; she was not leaving before they handed him his as well. She waited for his name on the PA system, but by the end of the roll call, which took another five to seven minutes, she still hadn't heard Paul's name at all.

"Do you think there's a mistake?" she asked.

"I don't think so."

"But he said we were all dismissed, all of us."

He looked down as though examining his shoes. "Will you forgive me?"

"For what?"

"They released me yesterday. No one really wants a lawyer in their jury box."

"So you lied to me."

"Yes, you could say that."

"And you sat in this very heat, and waited for me, and ate Tums with me when you could easily have had a real meal in one of your fancy Wall Street restaurants?"

"I wanted to be with you."

"You wanted to be with me," she repeated, pondering his words ever so slowly. "Why?"

"The honest answer? Because I want to speak to you, hear you tell me everything about your life, your parents, your patients, about the man from years back with whom you said you had an indiscretion," Paul said, using the word he remembered her using with him. "Plus, I love waiting to see you every morning at Pirro's. I think of you a lot."

"But we've run out of ways to see each other. We can no longer come here, no Chinese restaurant, no Da Pirro—don't you see?"

"Yes, I do see," he retorted, "but we haven't run out of options. First let's get out of here. I know a place where they serve wonderful Italian soft drinks. Chilled and not too sweet."

"What is the place called?"

He couldn't contain his laughter: "Da Pirro."

Together they walked out of the main waiting room. "This is the last time we'll see this place," she said.

"Miss it already?"

"Not the room."

"Let's not give up yet. We do have a few choices. We could just fly to Naples. Hotel Segreto. That's Plan A."

She shook her head. "Too chimerical!"

"Right. There is also Plan B," he said, "which might involve telling a tiny little white lie."

"Like what?"

"Like you weren't released from jury duty yet, and

still needed to appear tomorrow. I've done it, and as you saw, it wasn't too difficult to pull off. We'll both be truants. We'll have a picnic in the park. I know of a lovely spot, close but not too close to the tennis courts. We can have picnics there, as often as we wish. Our secret alcove away from everyone and everything."

"A picnic? Really?" She sounded disappointed, almost scoffing at the idea.

"Well, there's also Plan C. I can pick you up by car, and we'll drive to the beach. No one uses the house, we'll buy some stuff along the way and I promise I'll cook you a fabulous meal and we'll be together and then we'll see."

"What will we see?"

"That's Plan X. There was a time when Plan X trumped A and B and every other letter in the alphabet. Just bring a bathing suit and I'll pick you up by car."

"Sounds so louche."

She was right. He regretted even saying something like that, sensing that what he'd just proposed was spoken by the ghost of an old voice that was no longer his and had sprung from at least a decade earlier. And yet, raising the subject did not feel strained or make either of them uneasy, especially after she brusquely interrupted him and asked, "So what did you think of when you thought of me last night?"

He loved her candor, especially given the subject.

"Since you asked, last night I hugged you or you hugged me, as you did on the High Line, and then you kissed me. We didn't dare make a sound or move an inch, obviously there must have been someone else in our bed, but we didn't fall asleep, and maybe I was half-asleep myself and we stared and stared, not a word, and all I kept thinking is what would my life have been had I never met you, never asked about the book, what if this was like the new chapter I've been avoiding for so long? What if your hand was holding mine and you wouldn't let go because we were already making love to the rhythmic sound of the surf across my hotel room in Naples?"

"What do you think would happen if we did make love?" she asked.

"What happens if our day at the beach turns into a night at the beach?"

"What if by Saturday morning we realize we like who we are together and don't want to change any of it?"

"You mean," he asked, "will our spouses be surprised when we finally tell them what happened? The answer couldn't be simpler: they already know. How stupid do you think your husband or my wife is? If they don't already know, they won't be shocked. I suspect they can't wait to have their turn in our central jury room. Would you be jealous if they met someone whom they grew to like?"

She pondered the question for a fleeting second. "Not jealous at all. But I'll tell you what happens if you and I were crazy enough to do what you are suggesting. We'd do it once and never meet again. Would that be better?"

She was so right, he thought. She was right about herself and right about him as well.

"The problem with people our age," she went on, "is that we've lived through or imagined too many variations on the same scene and know where most lead. We know we should claim to know less than we already do. We even know better than to speak our doubts, much less to those who shouldn't hear them for fear they'd change their minds about us."

"Thus spake the shrink. And so well. So, one evening, as I was coming back from my squash club and you were coming back from the library, we might have met in the elevator.

"*Plans for dinner?*

"*Haven't even started thinking of dinner.*

"*I can whip up something real fast . . . maybe an omelet and a few other things?*

"*Wine too?*

"*Wine too.*

"*May I say maybe?*

"*Yes, of course, but the next chance lies forty years away.*

"*I can wait.*

"*We can all wait. But what a waste.*"

"We've lived good lives, Paul."

"Yes, but why didn't we meet back then?"

"We didn't meet because what made us so special, so happy to meet, was aging. Don't you see?"

"Don't I see what?" he asked.

"That we needed to be near the edge and almost dried of blood to welcome what we know can so easily be taken away from us now. Are we perfect? No. Are we good for each other? Who knows. Is this more than just friendship or is this Browning's love among the ruins? I can't tell. It's all we've got. Your office, my patients, our children, and of course our spouses—do they matter? Of course they do. But over and above them hover Heathcliff and Catherine, grown much, much older and carrying Medicare cards and senior citizens' MetroCards."

Pirro brought two canned sodas to their table, one blood orange, the other lemon. Chilled citrus was exactly what New York needed on such a hot day, he said. "By this time tomorrow," he said, "everyone will have left the city. I will close early, and I will meet my friends, and I don't want to think of anything until Monday. What plans have you got?"

"We haven't decided."

"On days like this, I love the beach, and Naples was my beach once. Now it's Fire Island, but only when friends invite me. So when are you going to Italy?"

"Haven't decided that either."

"Come on, people! Just think. You buy two tickets, you watch a few bad movies on the plane, you sleep poorly, but eight or so hours later you're in Naples, and you'll get in a cab and head straight to your nice hotel in Santa Lucia. I can already smell the beach, the air is crisp and clean—well, not always—and before you know it, it's time for a late lunch in one of these ancient *pizzerie* in the heart of old Naples. After lunch, you'll buy a *sfogliatella*, one for you," he said, turning to Catherine, "one for him—because a man without a *sfogliatella* is what kind of a man?—and of course one for me, and then you walk to any *caffè* facing the sea. The rest is up to you. Memorize the itinerary. Please go. But as I look at you now I'm starting to fear you will chicken out and not do it. If I see you again on Monday, I know you'll never go. And it will be so, so sad."

Just as Pirro finished his itinerary, Paul remembered what Catherine had said about meeting across the park one day and how the sheer prospect of meeting would seem so unwieldy and awkward that almost nothing, not even the strongest wish to meet, could overcome it—except for this other thing, which some have a lot of and some almost none left: faith.

He turned to her: "Do you trust we'll meet again tomorrow?"

"Do I hope, yes," she said. "Do I trust? I don't know."

"Can we at least promise to try?" he asked. "At our age, we no longer know if our hearts and our minds, to say nothing of our bodies, are on speaking terms."

They'd been sipping their sodas and had almost finished them only to realize that they had hardly paid any attention to what they'd been drinking.

"Tonight," Paul went on, "we might even decide to make light of the whole thing, and to convince ourselves that we no longer harbor the merest shadow of trust, we'll tell our spouses over dinner that we've met this very strange Neapolitan barista who strongly recommended a trip to Naples. *Naples, why Naples?* they'll ask. Because some crazy barista planted the idea, and going along was easier than arguing. *Fancy your going to Naples as a tourist now*, spoken with that unmistakable twinge of unkindness and derision that drives so many couples apart."

She heard him and shared every one of his anxieties. Then: "I don't want to go home yet," she said.

"I don't want to go home either."

What she added made them both chuckle: "We can always go back to the main waiting room."

"Do you think you would have liked me had we met that one night in the elevator?"

"Yes." There was something so certain and firm in her quick answer that it caught him by surprise.

"Why didn't we, then?"

"We never took the same elevator."

"Can you imagine if we had?"

"Fate had other plans."

"I don't want to agree."

She looked at him. "Actually, I don't want to either."

Late that night he thought of Hotel Segreto. They'd arrive there just as the barista had foretold. They'd open the tall French windows, step out on the balcony, and suddenly face Mount Vesuvius and the seafront and the blinding light sweeping over Naples, and they'd stand there under the punishing sun, leaning on the scalding stone balustrade, counting the seconds before turning inside, elated to be there. It would be so quiet at that early-afternoon hour that all they'd hear would be the twittering of the parakeets and the seagulls squawking above the rooftops. The two of them would need to freshen up and find a good cup of coffee to remove the taste of the syrupy brew they were given on their flight or on the train, hours before. Then there was the walk along the endless beachfront, then up to the monastery of Santa Chiara, because his mother used to sing a lullaby about it when he was very young. They'd walk till exhaustion struck, then much later, around seven or so, as he remembered from his numberless trips to Italy, the much-awaited *apericena* on the rooftop with pickled caper berries, before heading to a late-night dinner.

She thought along the same lines, no longer sure whether she was imagining what might happen during their trip together or remembering the Naples of an earlier stay with Jonathan. He was no fun to travel with, always complained about the weather, the dirt, the fact that no one spoke English, that everything felt wrong, dated, unwelcoming, and that people were forever prone to pilfer and cheat.

On her way home, she toyed with the idea of Plan C

and was surprised to catch herself actually rehearsing what she'd tell Jonathan. She'd find a way to say she might not be coming back that night, so he shouldn't worry or wait up for her—as if it were his worrying that concerned her. Had she planned to sleep over at their usual friends' place, she would have told him their names. But she wouldn't say a word about who or where, and he was a good enough shrink to put together the pieces and figure out the rest without saying a word. No need to lie about jury duty. In the morning, Jonathan and she would have breakfast together. He'd make her coffee in their espresso pot as he always did, she would fill two bowls of their complicated cereal, one for him and one for her, they'd take their time eating, then she'd pick up her bathing suit, stash it in her weekender bag, and would be about to head out the door when she'd turn around, kiss him goodbye, and ask him to remember not to worry if she wasn't back later the next day.

Had he asked where she was headed that morning, she'd have told him: someone she'd met in her parents' building, long, long before meeting Jonathan in graduate school. Where had they met again? he'd ask. In the central jury room.

It was the truth or, by now, its ghost or its shadow.

# Friday

*Tell me no regrets*, he texted at seven the next morning. *Not one*, she replied immediately, as if she'd been holding her phone all night. *You?* she asked. *None whatsoever*, he replied. *Meet me on 81st and CPW. 8:30 ok? Dark green SUV.*

She didn't respond immediately. Maybe she wasn't going to. Maybe she had had a change of heart. Maybe so many things. Why should that surprise him? She hesitated to confirm his text, and, because of the few extra seconds it took her to answer, he knew her reply couldn't bode well and might undo everything, even if she claimed to have no regrets.

Instead: *Why green?* It made him laugh. He liked her sense of humor. *My color. What's yours?* he replied. She didn't have one, she texted. *But maybe I have one and never knew it*. Then, following a pause: *Shrink talk.*

Maybe she was nervous. Or still undecided. It took him a second to realize he was too, nervous and undecided.

It had happened so easily and so quickly the day before. It had come not from his head but from somewhere in his chest or just below the chest. He didn't know where in his body, but he knew it was the body, and he liked that, a feeling he hadn't felt in a very long time but that sidestepped so many inhibitions he could so easily have shared with her.

After she'd told him she didn't want to go home yet, he had suggested they sit somewhere in Chelsea for a drink. He didn't know of any bars, but when he spotted one, they both agreed it would do. It was dark inside, and, without necessarily admitting it to each other, they liked that its wood paneling gave the room a dark and sheltered cast. "The wine will go to my head," she said. "Lunch was hours ago." "One glass of wine?" he asked, meaning to minimize the effect of alcohol in a single glass of wine. "I'll have one glass of white, then," she said, as though conceding to do him a favor. He ordered a gin and tonic. Then she changed her mind, asked the waiter to cancel the wine, she'd have a gin and tonic too.

"Still don't want to go home?"

She looked at him pensively and shook her head. "I so don't want you to go home yet."

As they waited for their drinks, the waiter brought three bowls, one containing peanuts, the next sweetened almonds, the third spicy mixed nuts. They were so famished that they didn't wait for their drinks to come. He suggested they not gorge on the snacks. Then, without really thinking what he was saying, he added that they should have dinner together.

"Do you think it's a good idea?" she asked as she found a lone pistachio in the bowl of cashews and began trying to shell it with her fingernails, then with her teeth.

"I think it's a very good idea."

She smiled as she finally released the pistachio. "It's a wonderful idea."

And because she had spoken so spontaneously, he couldn't resist following with something bolder and equally spontaneous. "I know what would be an even better idea: let's have dinner now."

She did not respond, thought for a few seconds. "What about the drinks?"

"Skip the drinks. The drinks can take care of themselves."

"So, this is another great idea from the man who never plans anything."

The waiter, meanwhile, was just bringing the gin and tonics to their table. Paul gave him his credit card. They didn't even touch their glasses and right away walked out of the bar and hailed a cab. "We'll order these elsewhere," he said.

"Where?"

"You'll see."

But the restaurant at the club was almost entirely empty, the air stuffy, and everything looked dated and lugubrious. He suggested going to the restaurant across the street, which boasted far, far better food, not the usual tired dishes they served here.

"I have a better idea," she said.

"Oh?"

She looked straight at him. "Room service," she said.

Her two words sounded so sudden and unhindered that they caught him unprepared. He hesitated, or was totally blindsided, maybe shocked, he wasn't sure which.

What he said came from a spot that reminded him of the ardor he'd felt just below his chest late that afternoon when he'd spoken his mind and suggested drinks, knowing that he was definitely upending their customary rush back to reality when separating at the entrance to the Eighth Avenue subway. He wanted to be as frank and exposed as he'd been then. "I need some prepping, I am prepping-less right now."

She laughed first, then they both laughed.

"I am no better. But we can be together, as we should have been decades ago."

She waited in the vestibule of the club while he obtained a room. In the elevator, they didn't exchange a word or look at each other. Once inside their room, she put both her arms under his jacket and kissed him on the mouth. "I wanted to hold you like this in the art gallery."

Neither let the other go until she began to unbutton his shirt.

"Unprepped, the two of us," she said as they embraced while taking off their clothes, and then, as though driven by an unforeseen sense of modesty, they immediately snuggled under the sheets in the light of the setting sun. Neither had thought of turning on the one bedside lamp in the room. He liked the long summer hours. She did too, she said. Both knew why they had rushed under the sheets. It made them smile. "But I can hold you better like this," he said, "and I can touch you all over." The two of them pressed together as they kissed and kissed again, just as he'd described how he'd imagined her in bed with him the previous night, staring at each other's faces, as they were doing now, with joy, and wisdom too, and the will to surrender far, far more completely than they might have done in their younger days.

"I'm so out of practice," she said.

"Same here," he said.

Both knew they weren't going to spend the night there. "I just wanted to know how you feel."

"Not going to be a one-off, I hope."

"Not going to be a one-off," she replied. Then, unable to withhold her laughter: "This is just the practice run."

They ordered dinner and a bottle of wine and right away held each other more tightly yet.

His dark-green SUV was waiting at the northwest corner of Eighty-First and Central Park West.

They greeted each other formally, but as soon as she buckled herself in and they were headed downtown, he said, "So here's a question."

"Ah," she said, bracing herself, without showing that she was expecting something serious enough to put her on her guard.

He hesitated.

"And the question?" she asked.

"Did you erase my messages on your phone?"

"Did you want me to?" She was answering his question with a question. "No, I didn't. Not this morning's, not last night's."

"I didn't either. But I know why I didn't."

"Why?" Catherine asked.

"Not because I don't care to hide anything, but because I don't ever want to forget what we said."

"What, making memories already?"

"I told you, I'm superstitious." He paused a moment. "Does he know?"

"He'll guess. And Claire?"

"If I know her, she already guessed the moment she overheard me call the cleaning lady last night to ask her to fill the fridge with food items. I told her I might spend the weekend at the beach. She didn't ask with whom. I said nothing. My silence said everything. And hers did too."

He had brought a tote bag containing two bottles of wine and enough food for snacks. He wanted to reach the house before the weekend traffic, he said. It was something to say to diffuse a whiff of tension and diffidence in the car. Then, gradually, the tension started to dissipate, but never entirely.

"Are we feeling a bit awkward?"

"A bit, yes. But to be expected." They both relished their frankness.

This was when he asked her to look inside a tote bag behind him. She turned around to the back seats, found the bag, and fished out a small pack of M&M's. It put them in a good mood.

They were not exactly uneasy with each other, although the whole setup felt like an official date, not the casual, improvised meeting that allowed them to feel perfectly natural each time they were thrown together by the court system.

In retrospect even their few hours at the club the previous evening had seemed more relaxed. As he drove, they managed to talk about a host of things: about how drab and ugly and defunct the area around the High Line looked in the old days when they'd catch a partial glimpse of it a stone's throw from London Terrace. She recalled blissfully leaving Twenty-Third Street when she got married and moving to the St. Urban. He told her he still played tennis in Central Park. Within sight of the St. Urban, he said. "See, fate kept trying to tell us something, but did we listen?" she said. They laughed. Sometimes, she told him, she walked her dogs to the tennis courts or took her grandson when his parents would allow her to spoil him a bit. "We love to watch the players," she said.

"We might have met there," he said.

"That was our rendez-vous manqué."

He liked that she had used his expression. He could tell that she was also ribbing him, but he enjoyed this coming from her, since teasing was, for both, a way of prodding each other with a harmless mix of malice, mischief, and banter to remind them that neither felt alone in the other's company.

"Have you ever had the sense that maybe all lives are nothing more than the chronicle of countless rendez-vous manqués, of stinging might-have-beens that continue to haunt us and, barring very few times, go forever unresolved?"

"Not all lives—but yes, most are unresolved. If I were cynical I'd say my bread and butter depended on this one thing."

"Which is why retirement is such a must," he said. "We need to get away from the same old tale and start reading the next chapter."

She mused on what he said. "Are you trying to tell me something, Paul?"

"I most definitely am."

Then she changed the subject. "And Naples?" she asked, interrupting what she felt had become a delicate topic, not realizing that the missing link between retirement and Naples was staring them in the face. Neither could tell if she was making a whimsical reference to their imaginary trip or whether Naples had become a metaphor for the undefined and unlived figments that the chance viewing of the painting in the gallery had stirred in them.

They were quiet for a while as he navigated leaving the city. She put her hand into the tote bag and, rummaging a bit without looking inside, pulled out a Lindt chocolate bar. "White chocolate!" she cried, with surprise. "I love white chocolate, I never buy it. Shall I break off a piece for you?"

He nodded.

"In case you haven't noticed," she said, looking straight at him, "this has been my best week in years. I'd forgotten what being with someone was like, and enjoying that someone. I've felt young and hopeful again—only to realize that I'd stopped being young and hopeful for so long. We keep repeating this to each other, but it's so true. That's the tiny joke time plays on us: it robs the memory of who we were and what we were once able to feel. As you said, we live with people but totally forget why we've chosen to live with them. Time and habit erase our reasons. There are entire weeks when I forget what another human being is for, what hugging does, to say nothing of that other business."

It made them laugh again. "Brought the preppings?"

"Totally *unprepped*. You?"

"Ditto," she said. Then, thinking again: "And I'll say something I've already shared with you: What I find difficult these days is being who I am, who I want to be, who I could become. I've turned reticent and withdrawn, selfless in so many things that don't matter to me, civil to a fault, but I feel cheated, addled, and, I'm beginning to think, damaged. Time does that as well. I may have so little to give."

"You gave me more than I gave you yesterday."

"Oh, you gave all right last night, Paul, yes, you did."

He turned to her for a second and rested a palm on the side of her face. "I'm so grateful we met."

"But Naples?"

He did not say anything, or was taking too long to answer.

"I'd love to go to Naples with you," he said.

But his answer felt evasive and irresolute, and though she knew she'd have been equally evasive had he asked her the same question, she felt sorry to see their tiny fantasy so easily dispelled and put aside.

"Will Naples turn out to be our rendez-vous manqué? How will I confront my patients on Monday morning, when I'll be sadder and feel more sapped of joy than they've ever been with me? And what about you on Monday, Paul? Won't you look back with sorrow on this week every time you recall asking what I was reading or when I asked your name and you said Heathcliff?"

"How could I forget?"

She looked out at long stretches of land on the right side of the highway. For a moment he looked that way as well, putting out his hand for her to take. She did.

"You have the hands of a pianist," Paul said.

"I do?"

He nodded. "Would you have spent the whole night with me had I asked you to?"

"Yes, I would have. But you didn't ask." She thought for a moment. "And to be quite honest, I am glad you didn't. There are so many things at stake, all of them possibly quite meager and frail by now, some downright insignificant. But we've built our lives with them and they are who we are, who we've been made to be, sometimes even against our will. Where would we be without them? Long way of asking, would today change anything?"

"I don't agree," he said.

She looked at him and smiled. "I was hoping you wouldn't."

They liked thinking along the same lines, filled with hesitations, rebuttals, and returns to newer versions of discarded uncertainties.

If it hadn't occurred to them until then, they finally saw it clearly: they liked each other, and these perpetual back-and-forths, easily passing for the tiniest brewing skirmishes, were nothing more than subliminal love-making.

"Maybe the way you state things," he said, "makes me want to disagree even though I was prepared to agree and to think the way you do. We're not dead yet, and we're not damaged either. But we are hurt. We're not trapped like people who've given up on their lives before even trying. It may be a cliché, but there are things I still want. I want to pick up my Latin and Greek again; I've never been to hear *Lohengrin* or *Parsifal*. I need to learn how to drive stick; I want to learn the Neapolitan songs my mother sang; I want to do unheard-of new things and I want to do them with you, and only with you. Without you they might as well all sink in the bay. Lunch at a Chinese restaurant changed my life. But what about opening our hotel balcony window and watching the sun rise over Vesuvius?"

"Lovely, yes. But fantasy, my dear. If I enjoy thinking of Naples too it's because it's unreal and no different from your Technicolor movie theater."

She looked at him and smiled again. "Maybe I dread change, though I too long for it. But then, is change what I really want at this point in my life? Is there even time for change?"

"Time is so insignificant. Has time ever been our friend? Haven't we lived by the clock, you for forty-five minutes each time, and I billing by the clock, and both of us being lied to and having to pretend we buy lies each and every time we punch our respective clocks? The young man who played squash in the evening is asking the young woman with the lava lamp to finally have their rendez-vous. He is still the same, she is still the same. There is no *Maybe next time*. There is no next time left. This is the next and last time." Silence. "There are two croissants, one chocolate, the other plain, in the bag. Let's split them."

"Do you know what I liked about the painting in the gallery?" she said after she offered him his half of the plain croissant. "It's the moment when you stared at the picture and said, 'I could just live in that room overlooking the sea,' while I thought to myself, *This guy! I could so easily live with him in that room overlooking the sea.* I wanted you to hold me and I wanted to hold you. I wanted us to be in that same room, wherever that room is. But you were such a fuddy-duddy gentleman. I knew I liked you, I just didn't know where this could go."

"And now? Do you now feel it could go somewhere?"

"I wish I were the type to say yes. As soon as I say yes, I start taking it back. I'm sure you've noticed."

"Some shrink!" Paul said.

They both remembered the painting. The narrow balcony with the wrought-iron railing, the open French windows, the shimmering blue sea.

"The Gulf of Naples," he said. "We liked it because it's the portrait of what might have been ours, the place where we're almost dipping our toes into the Mediterranean if only we'd go downstairs and cross the street before the shoreline gets crowded with all kinds of young bathers and rogue peddlers. Don't you see that our life will remain *manqué* if we don't go?" He was unable to believe that this was what he was saying. "Which is why it means so much. Every time we see this room with its open French windows, we know we belong there; I'm always alone in my imaginary rooms, but in this one, I'm with you."

"But can you handle regrets after burning bridges?" Catherine asked.

"Would I have regrets? Maybe, but what is the alternative? How about you?"

"Maybe right now, as I'm here in the car with you, no. I wish I could join you in Italy, I wish I could hear you sing your mother's song when you shower, and I wish we had found a tiny room in London Terrace where we might have made love so long ago. As for our Naples, it bears not only Pirro's signature but the very, very best the two of us could have given each other. I wish things in the past. And I wish them in the future. But I feel trapped in a present that isn't even mine any longer. I'm like the old Hungarian, whose past is like a ghost town and his future a shadowland of promises he means to keep but most likely won't."

"I don't want to become a mirage in your life," he said.

"I don't want to become one in yours either."

"Give me your hand."

She gave him her hand to hold, and he kissed it and didn't let go.

"I don't want to kill what we have," she said, "but I don't know what to do."

As they were driving through Long Island, he returned to the Hungarian's bench. "About the old man," said Paul, "maybe your mentor was right. What the old man meant when saying he wanted to be alone was perhaps to go back to a time before he met the woman who can't speak to him any longer, to a time before he had a son and grandchildren, before he'd even studied English or medicine, before leaving his homeland to come to the States. While sitting on the bench he was not thinking of the end or grieving over the state of his life. As absurd as it might sound to us, most likely he was fantasizing about a new life he didn't dare confide to anyone. The man wasn't giving up. There were things he still wanted. In a sense he was trying to go back to a moment when he hadn't taken a particular turn in life and, despite his advanced age, was thinking how to wind back the clock and live a totally different life in the time that was left to him."

"You may be right. But right now I like what's here. I love distant views of the sunny ocean in the morning, just as I loved staring at the Hudson and looking over to the old tower of the Erie Lackawanna station with you. I love that we are together right now. I just need time. What we have may not be enough for either of us. Or perhaps this vision of a new life is not for us either. I don't know. Meanwhile, Naples is not going anywhere. Naples isn't so far either. We have time. Will you wait, though?"

"Of course I'll wait. I want to wait. Now for another bite of chocolate."

They arrived at his house in East Hampton before noon. He checked the refrigerator and saw that the cleaning lady had purchased everything they'd need. Eggs, milk, sourdough bread, and so on. She'd even decided to buy three cans of tuna. He'd told the cleaning lady he'd leave her money in the usual spot on the kitchen table, under the mortar and pestle.

Catherine watched him slip the bills under the mortar. "An interesting antique," she said.

"It's not an antique," he replied. "It belonged to my mother. She liked coming here, and one year spent a whole summer in the house by herself. God knows why she needed a mortar and pestle. But for some crazy reason she had brought the thing from Italy. It was one of the very few things she'd lugged all the way to the States."

For lunch he managed to improvise something simple and delicious, using vodka and a bit of cream in the tomato sauce. He remembered that his mother would sometimes cook for him when he'd drive from his office on Fridays. He'd eat with her and then drive back to the city. He'd do it again in a flash if she were alive today. "My mother used to like it here," he said. "I think it's because of the water."

After lunch, and after brewing what Catherine referred to as the best coffee in the world, he suggested they take a walk along the shore. Had she brought a hat? She had brought a hat. And sunscreen? And sunscreen too. Good thing, because there wasn't any sunscreen in the house.

Neither wished to ask about putting on bathing suits. She was leaving it up to him. He was leaving it up to her. She started laughing; he did too, because he had immediately guessed what had made her laugh.

"Let's leave the walk for a bit later," he said.

"And see how things develop?"

It brought a sudden, expansive smile to his lips. "I adore you, Catherine."

It was midafternoon when they decided to go for their walk. They had even managed to steal a short nap and were in the best of moods.

"So," she said, after the two had put on their hats and sunscreen and had already walked past one dune and another, which he told her was a totally new dune, until they finally reached the shoreline. Her "So"—seemingly thrown out so casually—suggested a portentous *let the shrink ask now.* "So, tell me about your mother from Naples."

He looked at her with an I-thought-you'd-never-ask smile. "My mother," he began.

And right away, as they dipped their toes in the water, they knew that their walk would last a long, leisurely while. He started telling her of the war years, when his father was stationed in Naples and had met a local girl recently hired by the US army base. She knew just enough to be asked to stand in for one of the typists who was sick that week, but he was struck by the way she stared at the giant Remington they had placed before her. She right away confessed that she had never seen the letters *K*, *X*, or *W* before. They discussed the matter for a short while, but when she finally raised her darting eyes to tell him that Italian didn't have these letters, he knew immediately that those startled dark eyes of hers could stop army trucks in their tracks. Still, with the typewriter before her and both her girlish, thin hands resting delicately on her lap, she turned and said, "Captain Wadsworth, what would you have me type now?" He'd frequently tell the story of how they met and how when she asked him what she should type, all he could think of saying to her right then and there was "I've fallen in love with you and I don't even know your name." Her chilling response as she put back the cover over the typewriter, determined to walk out of the office, was simply *"Un altro!"* Another one!

He persuaded her to stay for the day. Then she stayed for the week. And then, fearing he'd never see her again now that the person who'd been sick said she was coming back the following week, he did something so bold that he knew one way or another it would change his life. He asked her to invite him to her parents' house for dinner. He would find everything they'd need, and more, at the PX. "But I have to ask my parents," she said. "As long as there's not another reason to say no," he ventured. "There is no other reason," she replied. It was the first time he saw her smile, and on that night she cooked dinner for Captain Wadsworth.

He was never the same again. When she was with her mother in the kitchen, he overheard her sing a song with a low voice, and, while her father was speaking to him in the dining room, he couldn't focus on a single word the old man was saying. He stood up, apologized for leaving the room, and walking on tiptoes, headed to the kitchen. He waited by the door for her to finish the song. When she was done singing, he asked her the name of the song. "*Dicitencello vuje*," she said, as though asking, what else could it be but that? Would she please sing it again for him. What, the song? she asked, totally surprised by so simple a request. Yes, the song.

And once she started to sing it again, she kept staring at him so intensely that he had no recourse but to start tearing up in front of her and her parents. It was my gift, she said when he stood at their door and was about to leave, long after dinner. Can I come tomorrow? he asked, knowing it was totally out of place to ask. She did not say yes, she said *a domani*, until tomorrow. It changed his life. Over the years, he'd still ask her to sing for him.

She would sing for him softly in their bedroom; she sang on everyone's birthday; she sang for him when he was dying, because he wanted to hear her voice one last time.

"Had Captain Wadsworth not dared to tell her so openly what was in his heart the moment he set eyes on her, had she never invited him for dinner at her parents', she would never have left Italy, I wouldn't have been born, I would never have sat next to you in the central jury room, and I would never have dared ask what you were reading."

"Couldn't you tell?"

"Couldn't I tell what?"

"I was happy you asked."

They walked all the way to where some of the houses became mansions, talking endlessly about so many things.

"Was she beautiful?" she asked.

"Very, even in old age."

"You loved her?"

"So much. But then everyone did. She was easy to love. She may be dead, but she isn't gone. I speak to her sometimes."

"How?"

"I don't know, but she comes back to me. We joke, I complain about things, *I warned you*, she always says, and warn me she did when she was alive. I never told you this, but each time I went to Naples it was always on business, and I never once made a point of visiting the home where she grew up, never reached out to relatives, many of whom I'm sure are still alive today. Maybe I didn't want to find out. Maybe I didn't feel strong enough alone."

"You didn't feel strong enough alone," she repeated,

as though she'd read his meaning in far greater depth than he had.

When was the last time he'd spoken about his mother, she asked.

His answer disturbed her more than it threw her off.

"Decades ago, very seldom," he replied. Then, as though to dissemble his unsettling answer: "Strange, isn't it?"

"Not strange, sad. Maybe you should still consider going, and not for business this time."

"I would love to—but not alone."

They kept walking along the shore while he picked up shells, then aimed them as far as he could into the water. They decided to turn back. When they finally reached the spot where the new dune had risen, she said she wanted to sit on the ground for a while.

"Why?" he asked.

"Because I want to see the afternoon sun with you. You made love to me today."

Her words moved him so deeply that what he was about to say stuck in his throat and left him speechless.

Then she added: "I want to catch many more sunsets with you." And, seeing he wasn't saying anything: "Do I have to spell it out?" she asked.

"As you can see, maybe I'm the one who was born yesterday."

"Clearly."

He understood her well enough, but couldn't bring himself to believe it. As he'd done already, he let his hand rest on the sand next to hers for her to put her hand in his, and she did.

"We've caught up with four decades, haven't we?"

"Who's counting? But yes." Then, with hesitation in

her voice: "Can we not go back to the city, not today? I don't want to."

"So we're staying. Easy."

"There's just a tiny thing left, and we both know what it is."

He looked startled. Obviously, she thought, he had no idea what she was referring to.

"It's about August."

It took him a while. "Are we this crazy?"

"We're going to have to be."

"Will it make Pirro happy?"

"It will definitely make him happy."

They smiled, but neither wished to laugh.

"I think it will make your mother happy too."

"Do you think so?"

"I'm sure it would." They were silent for a moment. "What was her name?"

"Everyone called her Ginny, but her name was Ginestra."

"Ginestra, what a beautiful name."

"It's the name of a plant. They say it grows on Mount Vesuvius. It survives the worst eruptions. But I've never seen it. She used to recite a poem about that flower."

"All these years . . . ?" she started to ask.

"All these years," he replied.

All these years he had wanted to know his mother's world, the world of her songs, of her parents, of old Naples and old kitchen utensils that traveled far enough to outlive many lives, on this side and that side, lives he'd never known of and longed to know now, though not alone, because he already knew he'd cry and he didn't want to cry, not alone, though maybe it was good to cry in this world of sunlit balconies and sunlit faces, and of stunning voices that could nurse a child to sleep, stir a husband's love, and, when he'd grown old, send him to the next world with nothing but grace and plenitude in his heart, a world where sunlight itself forgives and forgets and where bliss is a promise, even when unkept.

"I so wish my mother had met you."

Catherine nodded in agreement. "But I met you," she said.

"We should have met forty years ago."

"Can we just assume we did? We weren't who we are now."

"Could we have been so different from who we are today?"

"You're talking two generations ago. That's a long time, Paul. I don't want to be who I was then. And I suspect you don't either. Come, your coffee is better than Pirro's."

They stood up.

"Was this your way of asking for another cup of coffee?"

"Yes, but I was also starting to wonder about drinks and dinner. Remember, you owe me an omelet and a few other things, and wine too."

"How could I forget?"

*MARIANA*

You knew.

Of course, you knew.

You knew from the very start.

As I knew. But didn't want to know.

Because I was too scared to know what a single day would be like without you.

Because you lied, or almost lied. Which was like watching you believe your own lies, once I believed them myself, or pretended to.

You always lied.

There are days when I think you always had me fooled. From the moment you walked in wearing that oversized damp woolen coat at the welcoming reception for new fellows at the academy, to the moment when you stood up and the coat seemed much too large and heavy for someone so lank. It was a woman's coat, I found myself saying. *Is it?* you asked. The buttons were on the left. You thought for a second but didn't say anything. Then you told me how much it cost, and I could already tell you were lying. *Not a hand-me-down?* I asked. *Not a hand-me-down*, came your swift laughter. But you knew I knew.

That smile. A liar's smile when he knows he's been caught.

I tried to believe you. But I wasn't fooled. You weren't even a good liar. I just let you lie all through the weeks we were together. Because it was easier. Because I didn't want to upset you. Because no one I knew could possibly lie so much. Because I knew you'd run away if I called out so much as a fraction of your lies—which would have left me exactly where I am now: alone, squirreling away random mementos on a Sunday afternoon, the way a monk stores the rags and bones of those who might someday become saints.

I hate Sunday afternoons, especially in early winter, now that I've shut my window and sit here watching the light start to fade over the water. I hate how I've let you turn my life into a dreary, sunless Sunday that begs for twilight, because darkness presages a hasty dinner in the dining hall, a new week, the news maybe, a bit of chatter with fellows who've come back late from their weekend away, then sleep. I'm here for only two months; this is your second year here, you know everyone. Sundays I'm always alone.

What will I do with myself, whom to see or even talk to, where to go in this small, dead town where I hardly know a soul and fear running into you if I so much as stroll outside our compound, knowing you'll think I'm stalking, which, let's face it, I am, because I'd give anything to catch a glimpse of you now that you've been avoiding the dining room. Just one glimpse, just once more, as I keep telling myself—always once more with me, that's my sickness—I can't let go, even when I know I should and want to. I wish I had been born stupid; at least I wouldn't have known how to look into myself and find every little blistered nook of my subconscious laid bare like this, asking to suffer. I know there's a part of me that likes heartache. There's something so tangible in heartache, maybe even wholesome, trustworthy—when was the last time I've felt anything so real? Kindergarten. But does knowing this make me any less of a fool?

You could call me ten years from now and say you wanted to spend a measly half hour with me, and despite everything I know about you and every defense and bulwark I've put up against you, I'd still say, *Let yourself in, I'm home, please come, and don't change your mind, just come.* I remember looking down the staircase from the fourth floor, your huge, damp winter coat spiraling its way upstairs, and thinking, *He's in my life. He's in my life. I won't say a word, I won't ask, won't quibble. Let him do what he wants, say what he wants, I'll go along, he's in my life.*

I always used to turn my lights off at night. Now I leave them on—come whenever, you're always welcome. And when I turn off my light, I want you to know that I'm not sleeping, just pretending. I'm still waiting but don't want anyone to know, just you.

So, yes, I am stalking you, and not just in my thoughts, because you're always there, but also on the streets of this shabby little town, hoping to catch a glimpse of you, knowing that you're always with someone new, taking her to the movies at the parish church, because it's cheap—you with your to-go coffee cup, your coat, rolled-up cigarettes, and the yellow plaid scarf that was once mine, which is the only scarf I see you wear these days, and which I hope might make you think of me—sure it does, how foolish can I really be?

Still, I don't want to see you with someone new. Nor do I want you to see me alone. Both would hurt, plus I know how you'd snicker and turn to her and say, as you said to me once when we were just coming out of a movie on a Sunday evening scarcely a month ago, *Don't look now—but I dated her once.* And of course, your new girlfriend would turn around and look, as I did back then, and laugh at the poor girl who was carrying last-minute groceries, and was probably using grocery shopping as an excuse for loitering about town on a Sunday afternoon, hoping to run into you just one more time. I remember your smirk as she rushed by, humbled and gaping at the pavement as though looking for a hole large enough to disappear into.

I am that girl now, aren't I? I'm the girl who leaves some light grocery shopping for last on Sunday afternoons, knowing that all the grocers are closed here, except for one, which is how I know I'll run into you at some point. I want to. I am not ashamed.

So here I am in my room this Sunday evening, sorting through a pile of trifles that take me back to our days together and that I'm embarrassed to have stowed away, as though I already knew back then they'd be priceless keepsakes one day: ticket stubs, café receipts, two theater tickets, two ferryboat tickets, the salad dressing recipe you penned in haste for me, and of course the two photos you took of me naked. You made me pose. And I let you take those pictures. Why did I let you? Why did I like it? Whom will I ever share them with if not you?

I have no photos of you. Why didn't I bother taking

a simple snapshot of you with my phone—you reading, you in that huge wool coat, you sleeping with just one foot showing? Not that I didn't think to take a picture. It's just that I kept putting it off, there'd be a better time some other day, and that other day was pushed back to yet another and another, the way I keep putting off doing laundry, because my store of clean socks and underwear, like the store of our days together, seemed endless. But no one told me of my expiration date. *Time's up, dear, time's up.* What hurts now is not just the speed with which you flipped off the switch on me, it's the sheer arrogance of thinking there'd be a right moment. No one told me that the right moment had already come and gone. That's the one thing I never learned. I live with shadows, should-haves, and aging trinkets: the swatch from the T-shirt you ripped when you climbed a tree to free a balloon for a child, down to the can of tennis balls you left in my room one day. I've never played tennis, but I like their smell, they make me think of you, they're mine now. I kept them, thinking you'd eventually come to take them back one day.

I hoard everything, the way a child might keep sea-shells to remind him of an unusually lovely day at the beach he hopes might happen again soon. I hate these scraps that remind me you exist. I would rather you died so that I could mourn you, but I've stopped hoping. It's hoping that kills me, hoping that makes me write about you and coddle the mirage that if you have no one better tonight, then let it be me, might as well be me, I'd let you in, I'd pout, but it wouldn't last. You'd sprint up four flights, hesitate as soon as you walked in, remove your heavy wool coat, and finally hang it on the tilting coatrack by the door and dig out your cigarette-rolling contraption.

But you won't come, not for the tennis balls, not for me.

I am learning how to live with this crater in my gut. I am like those who are about to lose their sight. They learn to say goodbye to everything they see, one trinket at a time, day after day. You didn't give me time. One day I woke up and I was blind.

But then, just a few nights later, you reappeared and by showing up undid all of my paltry resolves. Everything I'd done to bar you from my thoughts, all the sandbags to avert the merest eddy of desire were knocked aside when I failed to hear you come upstairs and heard you knock at my door and all I did was throw myself in your arms, muffling what I hoped you didn't hear: *Oh my God!* You tore through everything, just like a flood, and I let you pull off my clothes, and all the while you were making love to me, I was thinking, *Don't be taken in, Mariana, he'll leave once he's had his fun.*

Those six to seven easy minutes made me feel like a recovering alcoholic thrown back to square one. I drank, got drunk, hated myself, and put my clothes back on, while all of my useless prosthetic little mantras lay strewn about on the floor. I start from scratch every morning.

You've got someone else now, you've always got someone. Just crack one of your insipid jokes and she's yours for the night. I was. You were already in your second year at the academy, I was on my first evening, but I remember the litany of jokes on that night. The first I didn't think was funny, but I laughed all the same; the second I'd heard before, but I laughed to please you. You were sitting next to me on a narrow sofa in the cocktail lounge, and while talking, you kept staring straight at me as though trying to decide something I couldn't quite figure out, then you touched my forehead and brushed my hair aside. And all the while I thought, *He's the sort who touches*, while I won't even shake a stranger's hand unless it's offered, and not always even then. But your way is to reach out and touch and do that thing with your palm on someone's forehead. It felt so effortless and unrehearsed that it took me a moment to realize not that it was a bold gesture between people who'd never spoken five minutes before, but that I liked it and that I wanted it done again.

Then you cracked another joke, and this time it did make me laugh because I wanted to laugh, which made you laugh as well, and you let your hand glide over my shoulder, over my waist, then pulled me gently over to your side in a move suggesting we were long-standing pals, which, of course, we both knew we weren't, but I let you think we could be, and besides, we were laughing, and all I was thinking was, *I don't have to do a thing, it's all in his hands*, and I loved letting myself go this way, all in your hands, my leaning into you a bit more each time, because I wanted to, because nothing felt more spontaneous. I loved how whatever you spoke about could be turned into comedy and how you exaggerated so many things to bring out their humor. I knew there wasn't a sprig of truth in anything you said, but I accepted it, figuring that this is exactly what's to be expected at a cocktail party in an artist colony. Besides, you found humor everywhere, and I liked that. *The man next to you says Wuth, not Ruth*, you said, *calls himself Wobert. But imagine if his name were Rodrigo or Rodrick*—which cracked me up so badly that I heard myself say *Wodwigo*, and then, catching my breath after bursting out laughing, muttered *Wodwick*. This was the first time I'd ever made fun of someone's speech before. It made you laugh too, and suddenly, caught by the naughty spell that brought us closer yet and gave a light, frivolous, complicit cast to everything that evening, I laughed with you, wanted to laugh with you, which induced you to repeat *Wodwick*, once, and then to whisper it three more times to my ear, closer each time, till your lips grazed my ear, touched my ear, and I liked this too. The word became the namesake for what was happening to us. His name, each time we saw him after that, was not Wobert but Wodwick. Poor fellow would put down his book to get up to drink water from the fountain in the garden, and right away you'd whisper, *Watch Wodwick dwink*, and I'd still laugh, he'd pick up his book, and it was *Watch Wodwick wead*. Your laughter was always so contagious. Days later, when we saw a picture of the founders of Rome as babies being suckled by a she-wolf, you couldn't help yourself and exclaimed in front of everyone, *Behold, everyone, Womulus and Wemus*. I think everyone knew what you were doing.

But then, just as I was starting to snuggle into our chumminess, you let go of me, and suddenly I found myself wondering, *Why did he let go?* Could it have been all in my head? That's the part I never understood. The jolt. Always the jolt with you. You skidded from laughter and that mirthful glint in your eyes to a midwinter scowl that made me fear I'd crossed a line or misconstrued our instant camaraderie for something it was not, which is why I gave in to you so soon, fearing you'd changed your mind, which is why the smile that sprang on your face soon after the jolt lifted the cloud you'd put between us. I said yes before understanding what you were saying. *Where do you live? Here*, I said. *Here, here?* Again with the joking. *No, upstairs, fourth floor. Upstairs, then. Upstairs*, I repeated, knowing I was giving you the answer to an unasked question, all the while pretending I was merely repeating a word you might have misheard, given the noise in the room. *Upstairs.* How unbelievably direct you were. And how direct I caught myself being as well. I'd never met anyone who'd made me say what I'd just said so freely. This was so easy, it felt like play. It was play. So I let it happen, wanted it to happen, and for a moment caught myself thinking that it was going to be this easy with every man I'd meet after you, unless, unless it was never going to be so easy or so natural again, because it had to be someone just like you, the jokes, the palm grazing my forehead, the sham fellowship that drew us together, the damp wool smell on your overcoat I grew to like so much. I said *upstairs* knowing that no sooner had I shut my door behind us than I'd let myself say what I'd told no one before. I wanted it unfettered and free, and I wanted it coarse and shameless, tell me what you love and I'll tell you what I want and I'll slip naked inside your coat while you're still wearing it till I choke with your warmth and sweat in your warmth, do anything, just help me shut down my mind. I had just set foot in the academy a few hours earlier, and here we were naked.

You expected a good Catholic girl from Middle America. I just wanted to be a woman.

It's not the Christian girl you hurt. It's the woman who can't spend a night with any man but you.

I've tried. It's no good.

The boy from my floor who can't pronounce *r*'s. You were right. He can't.

The older man I ran into at our tiny train station who

asked me how to buy tickets on the new self-service machine and then, when one thing led to the other, asked
me to dinner and more afterward, and I didn't say no,
because I wanted a dark room with a man, any man, because I wanted crude and coarse; all I found instead was
kindness and care, and I wanted neither.

Even the barista from across the street, tattoos all
over his body, savage, tender, and tireless, but not you.

All I think of now is you and your coat hanging on
my rack, and wanting to be buttoned up inside it with
you inside it as well, naked and dirty, the two of us, naked and soaked.

I have no shame. We held nothing back. What I miss
now is not just you. What I miss is not holding back.
It's me I miss, the me I didn't know existed and that you
pried out of me like a misshapen mollusk finally eased
out of its shameful little slough, because you didn't care
either, and I liked that you didn't care, because not caring is what I needed in our dark little world on the fourth
floor. This wouldn't last, we didn't care enough, this was
all beastly—and I threw myself headlong, boasting to
a friend on email that we couldn't find time to sleep at
night, caught dawn together, slept at dawn. I had come
alive.

A month now, and I already feel something has died
in me. My skin is dry again, I am listless all over, I feel
nothing, my thoughts wither, I have no thoughts. I can't
focus except on what I want to say to you. I want to fight
with you, and even then I never know what I'd say. I can't
think—everything feels encrusted; my voice smothers
words you made me moan once, and God did I love
moaning them to you, vile and breathless, short, clipped
words torn out of me and as easy and supple as an arm

slung over your shoulder. I seldom speak to anyone, yet everyone is so kind to me, so thoroughly mindful of the bruises they know I nurse in silence; everyone can tell, but no one could ever know the filthy me you tore out on the fourth floor, the me hurled to the rocks below from my balcony weeks later, the me who loves to say your name when I don't want to be alone.

All you had to do was touch me and I was someone else, someone I couldn't recognize but who I knew had waited years in the wings, silenced and tame in the world I grew up in. I may be nobody to you, and you may not care a whit for me, but the less I'm me, the more I'm me. I turned off the light in my room because I was still ashamed and didn't want to face myself, or think of what I was doing with you in the dark, but I also turned off the light because I didn't want to know what was to come, didn't want to think in the dark, didn't even want to ask what I really, really wanted from you but didn't dare ask. Who knew, who knew, I certainly didn't, that I could be so fierce and firm in what I wanted from a man and that I could drop all traces of the propriety that everyone saw at the cocktail hour to turn into the smuttiest person you'd ever gone to bed with. Because I knew it was dirty, because you were dirty, because I liked it dirty, because dirt freed me.

Some of us have our senses at our fingertips; I did not. I discovered mine through filth.

You made it so easy for me, I made it even easier for you. Neither even had to ask. Do what you want, Itamar, and guess what I'll do. In the dark we did nothing wrong. In the dark we didn't even know who we were. You spoke to me, I spoke to you, but who knew what we were saying, what we said didn't matter, we were like sleepwalkers who could not be held responsible for what we'd done in the darkest night.

I was so free on those days. And so were you. When then did it stop being play? When did it become distasteful or boring for you? And how did it change into this monstrous thing that eats at me with shame and then weighs me down? I think of you all the time, if what I do is even called thinking. I've become like a shadow. I rehearse the words I won't have the courage to speak one day. I mull things I fear I might do. I shun public spaces at the academy, but even shunning everyone is nothing but a ruse. I want you to ask, *Has anyone seen Mariana today?* And I want those who know why you're asking to feel they mustn't tell you that they have because, without necessarily siding with me, they wouldn't mind seeing you worry and don't want you absolved so fast. I try to disappear to be mysterious; you disappear because you've got someone else.

My friend writes and tells me things will eventually be all right between us. I tell him he's deceiving himself. *Why?* Because I know deceit. I've touched it, breathed it, made love to it, lived it, and the worst of all deceits is the kind that wears any number of masks, and lying is the least of them: the sudden absence that refuses to explain itself, the cold shoulder in front of others, the women who appear from nowhere and then disappear only to reappear with a different name and are seldom the same.

Late on Sunday afternoons I still go out to buy groceries I don't need; I trundle about when all I seek is you. When finally I do bump into you with someone, as I know I will, I feign being in a rush, expecting a call from home. Sometimes you'll even stop. *You're good? I'm fine. You? Very fine.* Light awkward chuckle. *Emily, Mariana. Mariana, Emily.*

And I'll take this little interlude instead of nothing, my minute of light after sundown in the evening. And the irony is I know I'll draw something hopeful in the way you'll introduce me to Emily, or Heather, or Wendy, or whatever her name is. I'll even catch that glint in your eyes that could easily mean, *I'd so much rather be with you instead, Mariana. I'll call you*, says the glint again, *may I call?*—asked with the slick candor and feigned diffidence of a street punk hustling a bystander waiting for the number 17 bus, the whole thing borne with an impish wink that could just as easily mean you didn't mean a word of it. Just tell me she's not better than me. *Is she better than me?* You'll look askance, think, then the blank stare: *Who knows, Mariana, who knows*, tossed with a rakish tilt of the head and that old familiar *Bye for now.*

And *Bye for now* is good enough on a Sunday evening when the whole town goes to die on tiptoes and the movie theater is about to close and even the corner café empties out. The unspoken *Bye for now* I invent for myself each time I imagine running into you, because it reminds me that even in a sky studded with never-agains, there's still a North Star called hope. Never again our first night. Or the wine bar on our second night. Or the day you came unannounced by bike and carried it all the way upstairs because you didn't want to tempt a thief, and you stood it near my bed and said *Take everything off*, and I did just that because with you there were no rules, yours were the only rules, and even if I knew that I was just going along because this couldn't possibly matter, and who could get hurt, who'd mind wasting a half hour like this, half an hour is all he's worth, poor little devil that he is, him and his coat and his bike and the smell of his armpits that takes me away from everything that's dreary in my life back to my earliest childhood when life felt so safe, so fresh, so new—just an armpit, did it matter that you were dressed and gone within twenty minutes, shouting a *Bye for now*, as I was back at my desk, leaking you, Itamar, Itamar, Itamar, feeling so safe, so fresh, so new, cleansed by what I'd once believed was nothing short of dirt. I worked so well that afternoon.

Did I know where all this was headed?

Not a clue. And yet of course I knew. How couldn't I have known?

Did you?

I doubt you even asked yourself or cared to ask.

There'll never be a *for now* again. That's the part that is so difficult to accept—the thought that from now on we may never touch again. I can't bring myself to believe this. You'll show up again—you have in the past. But those hasty twenty minutes on that one afternoon—who else but those who had all the time in the world could have squandered them so thoughtlessly without being more frugal or leaving spare little bits for the "lean days when." And now even the lean days when have come and gone, your voice is gone, and the scent of your skin is gone. I know what you smelled like and I'd recognize that smell in the most mobbed temple in Goa, where people can't even jostle one another and their smell hangs everywhere—but I can't remember your smell, or re-create it, and nothing, no one, not even when I refuse to wash so as to be able to smell my own body, can bring back that moment when you let me doze on your chest under the sun, and just inhaling you made me want you again and again except that, in knowing how close you were that day, I simply forgot to earmark the moment, the hour, the day, the month. The year, even.

When you live in the moment, you forget the moment.

And now I am also starting to forget your face.

The other day when you called, and I kept hoping it was you calling, I failed to recognize your voice. I liked that I didn't know it was you, because here was proof I'd moved on and maybe even outgrown you, which I hoped might upset you. But one minute later your voice was gone and I had no recall of it. And as for being slighted, what you felt, perhaps, was not the snub but relief. *This didn't take long—she's finally over me.* No guilt, no unwieldy lump that sits on your chest even when you couldn't care less whether I live or die.

But here is the story of the lump in my chest that never went away. For I still recall that one evening—it was a Sunday evening too. You said you'd come, so I waited. I waited all afternoon, all evening. You had promised. But I wasn't a child holding Daddy to his promise. So, all right then, so he won't come. I made myself an instant broth and sat down for work. *Enough with fun and games, let him tell his sordid little jokes to others, let them laugh together, I have more important work to do.* But I wasn't fooling anyone. I kept rushing through my work in case you did show up, even though it was now so late. But I knew I was waiting, because I kept putting off changing into my house clothes—my faded sweats, part pajamas, part the frayed sweater that everyone wears when they're alone. Every time I heard the door slam downstairs, I caught myself thinking it was you—and seconds later would berate myself for daring to hope, but still hoping way past midnight. *You have a life, Mariana*, I told myself, *you are very good at what you do, and you love your work*. But these were only words, and words in the wee hours of the night sit like craters in my heart.

But then, just as I was giving up, the door slammed downstairs, I recognized the stamp of your footsteps rushing up to my floor and then the knock. This was going to be the best night of my life. I was glad I had kept my nice blouse on. I was glad I had finished my work. Plus, I was free all morning that Monday. We were going to have breakfast together. You lay down on the bed with your clothes on, which forced me to do the same. *Oh, let him kiss me and have done with it*, I thought. You said you wanted to talk.

Suddenly, I began to sense where this was headed, and before I could do anything to alter its course after I'd started to remove my shirt, you said, *Put your shirt back on*, and I put my shirt back on, and I buttoned each mortified buttonhole, looking down at my blouse, feeling that, from the way you were speaking, there was actually no coming back from this. Something hurt, but I had no idea where or what the pain exactly was, or maybe it wasn't even pain, but like pain, because I still had no sense of the news you were about to deliver. Part of me wanted to know how or where to pinpoint it, thinking that knowing its location might dull its impact, but I couldn't locate it, having never experienced it before, didn't even know its name. But as I began to register the unexpected drift in your conversation, I could feel my entire being begin to sink—body, guts, brain, soul, spirit, and heart—in good part because I couldn't believe that what you were actually building up to was nothing short of an ordinary, flat-footed Dear Jane. I felt so trounced, so stunned that I wasn't even flustered or ready to shed tears, because I still couldn't believe and certainly did not know where all this was headed. I finished buttoning my shirt and sat upright on the bed and asked you not to speak, not to move, not to leave.

I don't know exactly what I was trying to accomplish, but I wanted to halt the course of whatever you were about to add, knowing it would inevitably turn that night, with the two of us lying fully clothed on my bed, into the worst night of my life. If I wasn't mistaking any of it and if the conversation was really headed in that direction, what I was really asking was, could you just rethink what you're about to say to me, Itamar, or walk things back a tiny bit, start again, think again, change that tone in your voice, or maybe even change your mind, Itamar, please, change your mind? I was trying to keep the last shade of dignity in my voice and my bearing, but I knew I was pleading—let's face it, begging—and in my tacit, timid way hoping you'd reconsider, which is when you finally turned to me with that baffled look all liars know to affect so well when they're finally cornered and about to be found out, and said, *What could possibly have put that silly notion in your head, Mariana, you couldn't be more wrong, come here, let me hold you.* You had just come to tell me you were leaving the academy for about two weeks, the usual short trip for an unveiling in Vienna, you added with a muted giggle meant to convey the negligible character of a small errand in Austria. Then you unbuttoned my shirt, and I faulted myself for misreading signs of what I suddenly realized for the first time in my life was my very worst fear: losing you. The pain I'd felt and that disappeared so very soon after you reached out and held me was in fact fear. By then, however, I had no recollection of it, couldn't even tell where it had started, how long it had lasted, or where in my chest I believed I'd spotted its whereabouts.

Online, while you were gone, I caught photos of you skiing. I don't know if they were recent pictures or dated last year, but on closer look, I saw in one of them that you were wearing the yellow scarf you'd once borrowed from me. I liked those pictures. I wanted to see more of them. I wasn't going to ask who'd snapped them.

You had shaved your beard. I liked you better with a beard, because the man I met at the party who took me upstairs to my room had a beard. The one you are now is not you. I trusted the mask, not the face. I trusted the ruffian, not the civil, clean-shaven artist wearing skis.

Hours later, more pictures on Instagram. This time you were with others, there were women in your midst. Maybe you had posted these images to send me a message. But I doubt you even thought of me. I knew I hardly mattered. Still, it hurt. And because it hurt I couldn't just let it go and decided instead that you wanted, you needed me to suspect that the images of you with women in the ski lodge were posted to keep me thinking of you. I knew you didn't care. But this was my last, imaginary hold on you, which was no hold at all, and I knew it.

It was late on a mid-October morning. The weather was still lovely that Tuesday, and I had the rest of the day off and was planning to take a book and an iced coffee to read on my balcony. I'd done it before, and I loved the stillness of the spot, the intense sunlight, the ripples just below the tiny cliff, and the scent of suntan lotion on my own skin, so unusual for that time of year. Near me, my beloved frangipani tree. I was going to skip lunch with the others—lunch was always a noisy business, and a good book on such a day was just perfect. All week I'd been congratulating myself for how easily I'd survived your absence in Austria. I was even surprised to find that I seldom thought of you, except with reluctance verging on relief and an incipient form of recoil, as though part of me was growing tired of you but didn't want to fess up to it, while another kept putting off remembering what we'd done together, for fear of finding I still missed you. But none of this was unwelcome. I was being weaned, I knew it, and I didn't want to fight it. I could almost touch how much I preferred a book on a sunny mid-October noon facing the water to having you in my room, especially when you would leave soon after we'd made love. But the more I caught myself welcoming the ease with which this newfound feeling of liberation had washed over me and seemed to release me, the more I forced myself to seek out feelings of contrition and remorse, as though guilt was the honorable price to pay for this sudden gust of freedom in my life. I could tell that I was already being disloyal, and that perhaps I had made it way too easy for you to go away for two weeks, that it was I, and not you, who liked autonomy more, and that it was I who needed to remain single, because I had always been single, and wanted to stay that way, especially with you. In the past it was never others who needed to get away from me but I who always found distance more desirable. I was learning something about myself that I wasn't too eager to accept or too willing to change.

But my edifice of intricate sophistries came crashing down only a few days later, during your alleged two-week absence, when I ran into you in the street. You were with one of your Ediths, Esthers, Evelyns. You were walking on the street, she on the very narrow curb, your hand on her shoulder. The shadow of an exiguous nod is all I got. No greeting, not even a glance.

Then I knew. I'd been lied to.

I should have trusted my first instincts when you arrived so late that night before Vienna and when I began to undress, you asked me to put my shirt back on. You'd come for one reason only, to tell me it was over. Now here you were with someone who wore slick leather boots and had long blond hair and you couldn't even bring yourself to say hi.

I turned around. You didn't. I wanted to call you later that day. But I didn't.

I stopped in my tracks and rushed back upstairs to my room.

When you failed to call or to appear at dinnertime, the message was clear enough: ours was a fling.

You see, it was not just your behavior but what was happening to me as a result of seeing you that completely brought me down.

I wasn't that surprised, so why feel so utterly undone if I wasn't surprised?

Perhaps because it finally dawned on me that not one thing you'd said to me was true. Nothing was true. What we had—did we even have anything?

To be fair, you never told me we had more than what was there. We lived separate lives in our separate suites at the academy. We just woke up in the same bed, and though we had meals with the others, we always sat together, and everyone knew. At night, I am sure, they heard.

The trouble could be that, though we both sensed this wasn't going to last, you allowed me to infer it might, and I went along, probably because I believed you more than I believed myself, even if my inference was my own doing, not yours. My fault, then, all my fault. I should have seen things more clearly.

And yet even this answer doesn't satisfy me these days. My reaction to seeing you with her that morning could not just be about truth. Could I be so foolish as to race up four flights and hurl myself on my bed simply because I'd been misled for a month or so?

But then, maybe there is something so damaging about deceit that it tore out my deepest beliefs—beliefs that had been put in place by those I'd grown up with and loved, and whose very words and faces were being tarnished by someone who did not value truth, and without truth, could there be trust, could there be anything? Days I remember at our log cabin by the lake every summer where no one seemed to lie, or needed to, where we cooked outside when the weather allowed and, with no TV, chatted by the fireplace every evening when it got cold, and sometimes my grandparents told stories of people who had died long before my birth but whose lives seemed to reach into ours, with a degree of levity and mirth because, however much they'd suffered and been bilked by fraudulent tradesmen or taken wrong turns in life, still there was a font of simpleminded decency in them that held a good handshake, a trusted look, or a verbal promise as a token of good faith and truth. And maybe, maybe, as I sat among them in the waning light of those long summer days of childhood, there was a side of me that suspected I did not deserve the hearth of truth and would struggle throughout adolescence to forestall my gradual banishment from a world that was nevertheless still mine. With you, though, I had met a partner who would either free me from my log cabin days or throw me back to remind me that, despite a few lapses, I had never really left them behind.

I must have fallen asleep, because the answer was hovering nearby when I woke up from my nap and saw that it was time for the usual cocktail hour before dinner. I had a mind to skip that daily ritual. I certainly didn't want to run into you with your belle, the two of you ensconced in the tiny sofa in the living room corner like two turtledoves who'd graduated from sidewalk-gutter bonhomie to our posh room with the dark damask curtains shielding the sun at dusk.

On second thought I decided to change, and it was while getting dressed that I caught my face in the mirror. I looked angry and pinched, not rested from my involuntary nap. And this is when it finally hit me: I could read it on my face. What I was feeling had nothing to do with trust, or with truth, or with deceit or duplicity or our old log cabin that I hadn't been to in years. It had nothing to do with pride either. These were all convenient alibis to avoid using the only word that mattered: *jealousy.* No one had misled anyone or lied to anyone, no one had coaxed or persuaded anyone to infer anything. No one was to blame. What I was feeling—and against this, reason and all my bag of quirky sophisms were totally powerless—was jealousy. It had a name, a color, a list of telltale features, and poor little besotted, foolish me was feeling nothing short of what drove Othello to murder or Swann to despair. I still did not know where the pain originated; I did not know what do with it, how to snuff it out or how to stow it away as when we hurl loose clothing under a living room pillow when someone rings our bell unannounced. One couldn't even reason it away. It was simply there, loud, loutish, and nonnegotiable, like a sumo wrestler sitting on a little child. I hated myself not just because I felt I wasn't good enough for you but also because I couldn't wriggle myself free from under the weight of jealousy. I wanted you back, I wanted you for me, I wanted you to love me and no one else, even if a part of me had always known that I didn't really want your love. I'm not in love with you, I'm not in love with you, I'm not, not, not in love, for one can suffer from the most acute bouts of jealousy without nursing an iota of love. I wouldn't even want to live with you, would never want to introduce you to anyone I know, least of all to my family, nor would I want you to love me or, worst of all, to have your children.

And then as I was going down the stairs, I finally saw that what I felt was in fact worse than jealousy.

I'd been abandoned.

Every one of my unacknowledged fantasies suddenly showed its face for a moment before fizzling out in shame.

Christmas in Paris—out the window. Renting an apartment nearby after my time was up here—gone. Summer together if we lasted that long—what was I thinking? Beaches? Amalfi? The log cabin? Ha!

As I walked down the stairs, something almost froze me to the spot. Everyone knew. How was I going to face them?

How to join the cocktail hour and not feel everyone's eyes upon me?

Still, I blustered into the large living room. I put on a smile, but not an exaggerated smile. No one would have been fooled by that, and there'd be more talk about the perky mask than about the glum face.

I wanted everyone to know that I knew you'd left me

for someone else and that I did care but wasn't, for all that, broken up about it. I wasn't stupid.

Instead, I wanted them to think: *She may be abandoned, but she's informed.* Abandoned but informed.

The words made me want to laugh, which gave my feigned smile a touch of honest good cheer.

What I didn't want was for you to see how I felt.

I knew you were bound to appear.

But you didn't.

And I was grateful for that. The last thing I wanted was for people to watch me react to your presence in the room, especially if you'd come with the blond girl.

Then I forgot and found myself enjoying the cocktail and looking forward to dinner. Maybe I had overreacted on seeing you with her that morning. Maybe you didn't matter so much after all.

With people in the dining hall, I managed to feign being happy, and feigning it long enough did make me happy. I tried not to look at the door. Instead, as I was smiling and being social with people I didn't particularly care for, I caught myself thinking of dying one day and of being welcomed by my dead mother, who is with her mother and her mother's mother now. I drew comfort, even pleasure, in self-pity, which helped to put you behind me.

But I was just throwing a small tablecloth over the sumo wrestler, and while I was making people laugh and caught myself laughing as well, I knew there was a side of me that was completely devastated. Still, I was in good company, the weather was holding up, and later that evening, after the vitello tonnato, which the cook had been promising for days, we all arranged to go see a film in the town's parish cinema.

After dinner, when I rushed upstairs to get my sweater, I tried to tone down this access of good humor, part of which I knew was probably affected and wouldn't last. I tried to recall how shaken I'd been earlier in the day and already knew that the anxiety was guaranteed to return once I was alone in my room at night. I'd never felt this before, never had a reason to mistrust anyone, never really been jealous as far as I could tell—or maybe just a bit, here and there. But that hand on her shoulder as she walked with you, sidestepping the gutter, that was a photographer's dream. You looked like a movie star and she was young and she was beautiful, and she was looking at you even as she was speaking. It was clear you'd been together for the time you were gone.

I wanted to be her.

I didn't want to be me.

I wanted to go to the movies with you, and God forbid I should see you there.

Why did you like her?

What I discovered about jealousy was something I had never expected: that whoever you were with me was not who you were with her, and that I didn't know, might never know, who that someone else was whom I'd never met before, and that I wanted him to be with me now, I wanted to know that someone else—what if I liked him as well, what if I liked him more than the person you were with me? Who were you when you were not with me? This is what killed me. What were you like with other women, what did you tell them that you'd never told me, what jokes, what subjects, what did you do together that you'd never done and wouldn't do with me?

As we were headed to the theater, I heard one of my

friends say that someone had come from abroad and was visiting the academy. *What's his name?* I asked, knowing exactly what I was doing. *Ekaterina. She's Russian.* You'd once told me that you'd been to St. Petersburg earlier this year. All this made perfect sense. In the theater, I sat next to Robert, with Cornelia on my right, and next to her Ralph. During a moment of tension in the film, I reached for Robert's hand. Knowing how I felt about you, he must have thought I had mistakenly reached out for yours. So he didn't really respond. But I left my hand in his, and he must have known at some point that it was indeed his hand I had meant to hold. Happens all the time in these artist colonies. Part of me wished you'd been in the theater watching this. Part of me wanted someone that night, anyone really.

Robert turned out to be a good man. He didn't make me forget you. He kept me company, and he was more than considerate. *Do you want me to stay the night? Do you want to?* I asked. *I will if you really want me to.* Totally unexpected civility after lovemaking, especially when I remembered how you and I had laughed each time we said *Wodwick.* I'd never met any man so sweet. Even his lovemaking was sweet. But he wasn't you. I remember how you held my head. No one had held my head before, I loved having my head held. How would he know that this is what I wanted, that this is what you'd taught me about myself?

*Didn't you know what I was?* you finally said to me when I made a point of running into you several days later after breakfast. We were on the patio leading to the garden below, and I had a sense that you had spotted me coming your way and meant to change paths, but failed to do so in time and then pretended you had stopped and were actually waiting for me. I had planned to speak to you, just to reconnect—as former lovers, former friends, former whatever. Not to make a clean breast of things, nor to confront or reproach you, much less to plead with you. I just wanted to speak, and not let silence chill the air between us so that in another week we'd end up avoiding looking at each other, like strangers with nothing but bile and venom in their glances.

Did I want friendship? No. An explanation? Not even. An apology? We're beyond apologies. And yet no sooner did we stop on the patio than out came the last thing I'd ever meant to ask: *Why?* This was not what I wanted from you, nor did I want you to see me as the whiner who traps her former lover, begging for a postmortem to hear why she isn't loved, what she did wrong, what she should learn. Is there ever an explanation? Is there ever a why?

So, yes, I found out who you were. Was I surprised? Was I shocked that you lied? Hurt, maybe—but not shocked. Shouldn't I have known better than to sleep with the first stranger I met at the academy? Maybe. What had caught me completely off guard was being sought afterward, day after day, night after night, then your disappearance, then your return, then your second disappearance and return. The times I spent on tenterhooks could fill ledgers.

There was so little left to say, especially now that you finally admitted you were forever unreliable and were not likely to change. But then you asked, as though what had happened to the two of us had happened to two strangers with whom we hadn't the slightest thing in common, if I'd be foolish enough to do it again knowing who you were and where this could head.

And here—God bless you, Mariana—I spoke the truth in a way that left you totally bewildered and rudderless. *Yes*, I said, *I would. And in a second.* I'd never been so outspoken and direct in my life, and may never have the boldness to do so again, but I was left no less speechless by your question than you by my answer. *After it was obvious that I couldn't make you happy? After you knew I desired others, many others? After I neglected you the way I did? After I put off coming to see you until it was shamefully late one night and it wouldn't have taken a genius to know where I'd been beforehand? Yes, despite all that,* I replied. And then I said something that I can't believe I said, but I know I meant every breath of it, at least in the saying of it during our walk to the garden: *I'd give you everything I have for one night like our first.* I don't know whether I was exaggerating, but I felt wonderful saying it. I even repeated it to you, and believed it even more when I repeated it more than once. I knew I'd regret it, and I knew I'd never live it down, and I'd die if people here found out, but right then I'd have done anything for you.

You listened, I thought with incredulity at first, then with pity in your eyes, pity for this poor, desperate Mariana. But what you said came unexpectedly: *Just listening to you makes me hard*, you said.

I knew I was going to regret this, but I wasn't going to let the moment idle away. I was expecting some form of drama-speak from you. But you were silent.

*Now, here?* I said.

*No, upstairs.*

I knew exactly what I wanted to do.

I was going to fight you, I was going to be difficult, I was going to hurt you with my teeth, I was going to be savage because that's what you'd brought me to, and I was going to hit you, and if you hit me back, I'd fight you, because all I really, really wanted was for you to hold my head as you'd done each time, with tenderness or with fury, I didn't care which, so long as you held my head, because that would make me shut my eyes and throw everything aside, who I was, who you were, why I had come, where I'd grown up, what I was doing here, why I was so angry. I just needed you to hold my head and ask, *Why do you fight me, Mariana?*

*Because I don't want to lose you.*

Afterward, as always, you left.

No promises.

No niceties.

No flowers?

No flowers.

When I saw you at lunch just a couple of hours later, you gave me the most elusive smile that wasn't a smile. You were wearing the same shirt, same dungarees, same sneakers, as always no socks. You hadn't washed. I hadn't either. I knew why I hadn't. I wanted every trace of you to stay with me for days. I wasn't even going to let them wash my sheets.

That's one of the reasons why I couldn't put you out of my mind. Your smell was on my sheets. I tasted you on my skin. I fell asleep as I'd done the other day, from exhaustion, from rage and shame and an overpowering sense of plain sadness. Sex had made things worse, so I wanted more. I knew I was losing my mind when I woke up not five minutes later. I knew it was crazy. Yet I had to do it. I got up and went straight to your room on the second floor that afternoon. *What is it?* I didn't care whether you wanted to or not, whether you were busy with work or you weren't alone in the room. *Just hold me, just hold me.* And, poor little man that you are, you held me. *Not like this,* I said. You knew. *I have to smell you. But I have work. Two seconds and loosen your shirt.* I had what I wanted. I rubbed my whole face in one underarm and then in the other. This is what I wanted, this is all I ever took from you.

I was about to walk out when I saw that the blond girl from St. Petersburg was in your bed. She was reading a magazine, totally unfazed, almost as though she was relishing the scene, relishing my despair.

*Thank you,* I said as I approached the door. And, turning to her: *Do svidaniya, habibi.*

*This is who I am,* you'd said. *This is how I am.*

And for the first time I thought I picked up a note of sincere apology in a man who suddenly seemed so much older than his years, if only because you finally realized the kind of bastard you were. But a good soul, all told, one who'd never been intentionally cruel to me.

You were simply not in love with me. I couldn't blame you for that. Perhaps, in your own clumsy, misguided way, you'd even tried to cushion the blow for me, the way most people do, by distancing yourself at first quietly, then furtively, finally by lying. I understand this now. Which is why, after I shut the door to your room and faced the large window in the corridor overlooking the garden where we'd met just after breakfast that morning, I not only realized that I had to move on and stop thinking of you, but also, with the door permanently shut between us now, this was probably the first time I knew I had fallen totally in love with you.

Late one night, I don't remember when, I called you, because I couldn't stop myself. You were too drunk, you said, and it made us laugh together, because I too was drunk enough to call you that night. I didn't ask, you didn't offer. We just giggled, not like kids who had crossed a line, but like grown-ups who could no longer dare to. Or so I thought.

Two thoughts. And I'm not sure which came first or how they're related.

One is obvious enough: *I don't want to go back to how I lived before, to who I used to be.*

My log cabin days are gone forever. I don't think I can actually remember them, or at least they've lost their poignancy, their meaning, their pastel radiance filled with the scent of mothballs, cedarwood, blackberry and cherry jams, and old people humming old songs, all points of reference from which one could plot the itinerary of one's life, as my brother and my cousins still do when they go back for a few days every other summer to recharge. But after you, I'm someone else now, and, as happens in so many cartoons, the large log cabin has folded itself into a minuscule wad of memories, the way we fold and cram tons of old shirts in a drawer we know we'll never open again.

I don't want to go back to how I lived before, to who I was, to who I've become after you. I want to be who I was that first week, in those wonderful few days when you literally made me fall in love with myself. There was something so sudden, so savage and spontaneous, so unschooled in what we did together. We were unleashed, unfettered, untamed, unashamed—maybe because I never trusted you, or couldn't take you seriously, or didn't think highly enough of you. You were my bed partner. But you were not part of my life. You taught me nothing about myself I didn't already know and brought nothing I didn't already have. You were just the agent, the spur and the goad that told me I wasn't wrong about myself. I didn't know I could actually be the person I was when I was with you—the woman who finally knocked at your door and asked you to loosen your shirt and then stuck her face into your body as if she were a wilted, desiccated cactus desperate to slake its thirst on a man's sweat; the woman who asked you *Ask me to take my clothes off* on the very night we met, since you wouldn't have thought of it yourself, the woman whose head you held as though it were a fragile glass ball and whose soul was yours to borrow, take, or steal because you waited, and waited, and waited for me and made me think—what did you make me think I was, you dear, dear man? I would have wanted you gone the next morning if you were like the others. But I would have snuck into your coat pocket and gone away with you wherever. Was I in love with you even on that first night and didn't know it? In love the moment you sat next to me with that big coat, and all I could think of was *I can smell him from here?*

I'm someone else now.

Do I like myself, though? No.

The other thought is more complicated. I was thinking of my death, and my death made me sad, not just because I'd be dead or because there are those who'd grieve for me—you wouldn't, I know—but because once I'm dead, I'll never have you in my thoughts, won't even remember you, or ever hope to run into you one way or another, not just now, tomorrow, next month, but in the years to come. Once I'm dead, you'll be gone from me forever. And that thought is unbearable. I cannot die.

These were my two thoughts. I don't want to die. I don't want to lose you. I don't want to go back to who I was before. I don't want you with me. But I don't want you without me. I repeat myself, I know.

I was trying to think that one day I'll be able to meet you somewhere, not at the academy in the days or weeks to come, or elsewhere in Europe, but far, far from here, and entice you for a cup of coffee. *I'm happily married now. And you are too, I hear? Yes, I am.* And surely I'll want nothing from you then. All I'll want is to tell you that despite all that's happened over the years, and all the happiness that life has brought me, the thought that you're not standing somewhere on planet Earth is un- thinkable to me. I may not reach out to you, but I need to know you're there, even if I'll never see you again. This, and not a thing more, is all I ask.

Right now, I may grow to hate you. But I don't want to hate you. I've run out of ways to forgive you, yet I'll al- ways forgive you. I think angry thoughts, and in my head I am constantly bickering with you, proving things that I know can never be proven, reproaching you for reckless misdeeds I've been guilty of with others, and may commit again. Jealous? I hope you are—if only a bit.

I like what I'm feeling today. But I know it won't last.

I've had my small instant of revenge—and in front of your girlfriend—but even that won't last, because the pleasure of getting back at someone never lasts long enough; besides, mine is laced with humiliation—I was so hysterical in front of her. What is her name? Ekaterina,

Ludmila, Natalya, Tatyana? And she reads magazines! Shame on you.

Something in me still wants to see you suffer, as I saw you suffer that day when you climbed the tree to rescue a child's balloon and ended up tearing your shirt and cutting yourself above the elbow, and I took care of your cut. *You deserved it*, I thought, feeling a tinge of pleasure in watching you bleed. My revenge for not knowing where you'd disappeared to two nights in a row. Then, as always, I felt guilty for not feeling sorry when you bled, and, as a result, wanted to forgive you for an absence that rankles in my mind still today.

I wonder what the two of you did when I left your room that afternoon. I walked down the corridor fast because I didn't want to hear your comments or how you both tittered at my expense once the door was shut. I could just see her aping my voice: *Take off your shirt, Itamar*, and right away she'd nuzzle up to your chest and then your underarm. *I am Mariana*, and both of you would burst out laughing. *I am Mariana. No, I am Mariana*, you'd say, imitating my voice.

I was so enraged as I left the building and walked around the main garden, stamping over my dearest frangipani blossoms, which none of the gardeners had swept away that morning, that I finally decided to slip a note under your door. I wanted to tell you that you were an ace bastard, that you had definitely ruined both my stay here and the project I was working on. I was also going to tell you that I am resolved never to speak to you again, never to look at you, and whenever I can I will show my hostility in public, especially at lunch and dinner in front of the other fellows. A part of me wanted to make up a story and say that on my very first night at the academy you got me drunk, then forced yourself on me, and that it had taken me two whole days to recover and I still can't remember what we did that night.

But as soon as I stepped into my room, the words I was going to write took a more sinister turn: *Thanks for the armpit, I needed that. I have good memories, but I don't think a friendship is possible any longer, regardless of what you led me to infer the other day. Friends have their tussles, but what we ended up sharing was far less than friendship. Ours are different worlds, and I can't see how they could ever meet, though a part of me might have wished they could. It would be too foolish and clumsy for you to yield to instant urges, as it would be for me to respond to yours. Things could have gone in a different direction, and there were times when I thought they might. But despite my sincerest wishes, my friend, you have to be cautious, as I know I must be as well.*

I wanted your beloved Russian mermaid to pick that note from under the door while you were in the bathroom and read it while hiding her fin and scales under the blankets. She'd learn that the woman who had come to smell your body one last time was letting you know she'd grown more tired of you than you knew. Then, after she figured you'd been dropped by someone who didn't want to say it outright, I tried to picture her resentment, aimed at you this time, not me. I imagined your rough, quick knock at my door, and before I'd open it, you'd shove it open yourself.

*Why did you send me this note?*
*Because someone needs to speak the truth.*
*Was that the truth, then?*
*No, not entirely.*
*Explain.*

*There's no explanation. I played you—and you're such a fool.*

*How a fool? I could just spit at you.*

*Spit on me and see what happens—so why are you hesitating?*

*I can't.*

*Why—not man enough? Want me to spit at you instead? Come closer, and I'll show you what spit can do.*

Why is it that with you nothing was forbidden? It couldn't have been love, certainly not the love of poems and songs, nor the love of the fishmonger lying in your bed puffing her gills as she gawks at you with fish eyes when she goes down on you. Why is it that no one else can do what you do when all you did is what all men do, and do it so poorly—the man in the train station, the barista with so many tattoos you couldn't tell his knee from his scrotum, and good Robert, who's remained a dear friend. I shut my eyes with them, imagining it was you, and it was easy to believe it was. But it wasn't you. Is it who you are before bedtime? Or after we've flounced to orgasm? Not even. One gave me so much more before sex; the other stood up paunchily naked in his little apartment, went to get me a glass of lemon soda in the kitchen because I said I was parched, and brought the glass with a little saucer, as my grandmother used to do. The man cared. You didn't. You said you loved me, yes, we all do as we near the pinnacle. Then we each find cunning little ways to take it back. To be fair, you never took it back. Because it didn't mean anything, because some people mutter obscenities during the act while others mouth sentimental claptrap. It's not that I believed you—I never did—but without knowing it you opened doors I had kept shut since who knows when. You had no idea. And the truth is, probably I didn't either until it happened. Until I realized the biggest fact of life: that I could never live with you, never have a thing to say or do with you, but that without you, life was just a barren little garden where the frangipani flowers I've grown to love so much here could easily be trod underfoot and would never utter a cry. I wanted you, God knows why, every night, not every other night, or every two, three nights—I wanted everything you had, and if spit is what you had, then spit it would have to be.

What you said in bed did not matter. It might as well have been a lie, a conceit, something like an orgasm of the mouth before the real thing. Or just a joke. The way you joke about everything, including me with the fish lady as soon as I'd left your room.

Mimicry is your strength, which is why no one dares argue with you here. You'll mimic their speech and they'll be instantly silenced.

One evening you mimicked everyone around the table and finally mimicked me. Everyone laughed. I laughed as well. You caught aspects of me that I thought no one had noticed. There were ways of speaking and facial expressions that I didn't recognize but immediately realized were indeed mine. Then you imitated Wobert, and said his name that way, and the good man laughed with his usual stentorian cough. You even mimicked the cook. Then Luisa, who works at the academy. We all laughed. But she did not laugh. I think she was hurt. Because, maybe without meaning to, you had crossed the line between mimicry and mockery.

When I saw her the next day, I asked if she was upset. What she said surprised me.

*This is who he is,* she said. The girl is in love with

you and you're probably not even aware of it. When you mimicked her, you almost made her out to be a supplicant nun. Maybe that's why she was hurt. And yet, of all of us at the academy, she is the only one who's good for you and you've never given her a second thought.

Luisa said you hadn't changed since your first day here last year, and will probably remain the same for the six months to come, which is well after I leave and am as good as dead to you. There'll be a time when my room will be someone else's, and who knows what you'll think when you'll happen to climb to the fourth floor.

Now that I think of it, I wonder who had my room before me. I asked you once. You said you didn't know. I should ask Luisa.

It's strange how I've started measuring time these days, not with my regular calendar, which always reminds me that my stay here is about to end, but by what I call Itamar Time. Life Before, Life After. Life Before means so little to me now. All those years with never a clue or the vaguest hint that they were all leading up to you. I don't want to think that someone like you could have hijacked the trajectory of my life, but when I look back, the days and years before you seem so threadbare, so scarcely premonitory of what was to come when you and I trundled down the narrow sidewalks of this small town and I thought to myself, *Everything finally makes perfect sense to me*. There was no dress rehearsal for you—for us—no premonition of what was to come even when I landed in Malpensa and took the train from Milano Centrale to here, not even suspecting that the jet-lagged girl from my log cabin world would, within hours of arriving that very evening, be sitting next to a man in a huge damp coat, wanting to snuggle into it, naked.

I can no longer remember my years before coming here without superimposing the view from my balcony overlooking the water, you sitting and drawing in the sun, me reading, our feet touching. You used to like my balcony because your room didn't have enough light, you said, and you liked to come here to draw. These days are not just part of my life; they've upended my life. Life After Itamar—when everything we did together could so easily slip into the past and become an airy, fluttering image no different from those very images I failed to anticipate when I sent in my application in bad faith, because I really wanted to be in Rome instead. Month 1 after Itamar, where will I be? Month 5, who will I be? Will I still long for you in Month 11? How about Year 2, when I am far away from the academy? How will what we had, if indeed we did have anything, loom in my memory? Will I remember this room and this very bed where I'm writing all this now, and think of everything here the way I think of my Sunday evenings here, when the town shuts down and life is turned inside out like an empty pocket with nothing but lint inside? That's how I feel, lint in my heart—all is lint these days. You're the empty pocket my life has become.

Luisa is different. *It's hard on us*, she said, meaning the staff here, *because we grow attached to some, and then must let go and think of the new fellows who arrive every few months or so.*

She sounded like a devoted nurse who gets attached to her patients, young and old. A nun, as you said once. All charity. But despite his wisecracks and bad jokes, Luisa says, everyone likes him. She's obviously trying to keep her distance, but I can tell that she pines for you, and in a way that I find quite touching, almost admirable, because it is so totally without malice or guile or the shadow of a grudge, as though she'd do anything to see you happy, which is probably a definition of love that is way beyond anything I am capable of, because she is unremittingly selfless and forbearing. *You like him*, I finally told her when it was clear she was trying to steer the conversation away from you. *Yes, I like him too*, she said. That *too* stung me. *She knows*, I thought. Then she changed course. *But he is too dangerous for me. Besides, I'm not for him, he's not for me.*

*How do you mean too dangerous? Too dangerous as in out of your league or as in someone not to be trusted?*

*But aren't the two the same?* she asked.

*They are the same*, I thought.

She looked pained for me, pursed her lips. *It will pass, Mariana.*

What generous and lenient words hers were. I had to ask her. She replied frankly. She'd always loved you.

Her answer didn't jolt me, didn't upset me, I wasn't even jealous, maybe because hers was love and mine wasn't, or because hers existed on a far purer plane than mine. Why hadn't I realized this about you and me? I'm not for you, and you're not for me. Why am I avoiding facing this?

In the end, it was her delicacy and her tact I envied most. She never overstepped her bounds, and much as I tried to get her to tell me, I never found out whether anything had happened between the two of you. Maybe something had, but she had enough foresight to put a halt to it before getting hurt. I never had such foresight.

I wanted to tell her what I was feeling these days, which was really another way of complaining and of opening the way for both of us to speak ill of you. She had, I was sure, her own litany of grievances. But she shook her head and changed the subject. She doesn't bad-mouth those she loves. How noble!

The only other time she spoke of you was a few days later when she came to my room and said that I'd been missed at lunch. *People are starting to wonder.* I told her I wasn't too hungry these days. *No, you and I both know this has nothing to do with hunger, but you must eat.*

*And besides,* she added, *the Russian girl is gone.*

You don't deserve her, Itamar. I could never make you happy. Luisa might. You just need to grow up.

But that's the difficult part. You're the most lovable person in this whole town, and your ability to let everyone feel as though they, and only they, matter when you're talking to them is your strongest suit. Plus, you are handsome, and your smile, which for some reason you know how to maneuver, is simply the most disarming thing you have. You're so present, and so unbelievably available to the person you are speaking with, that it's impossible for her not to assume that you want her to take that frisky dimple on your cheek when you start to laugh and own it not just for a night but for the rest of her life. I saw you at the tobacconist buying a pouch of tobacco from the girl behind the counter and smiling as you asked to purchase a new lighter—no, not the blue, but the crimson one, your favorite color, which any idiot could tell was your way of asking her which was hers. Or the time when we had a glass of wine on our second evening and you placed both elbows on the small table between us and rested your chin and cheeks on the upturned palms of your hands and asked me about summers growing up in Grandfather's cabin facing the lake, and all I could think was, *Why talk at all, all I have are his eyes, and I want him just to look at me*, until I suddenly realized I wasn't hearing a word you were saying—I believed I was the most special woman on the planet. Others may be in love, and doubtless we were no different, but during that moment in our tiny wine bar you made me think you had reinvented what love was—and to think, I kept telling myself, that only last night he was staring at me in the same exact way and I couldn't even spell his name, much less did I know what his surname was. Oh, and then the time one evening when you told me to walk behind you as two skinheads clearly looking for trouble were headed our way. They stopped you, one in front and the other starting to come behind you, and suddenly you punched one in the mouth so hard that he fell to the ground while the other immediately fled. And standing above the one lying on the sidewalk who was already bleeding from both mouth and nose, you took out your cell phone, snapped a picture of him, and asked if he wanted you to call the police or an ambulance. With his hand, he waved away either option. You called the police. They showed up and even recognized him by name. What I liked about the scene was not your courage, or how you told me to walk away from you and moments later to stay away while you snapped several more pictures of the skinhead on the ground. It was the absolute foresight with which you knew there was going to be trouble and had already anticipated what you'd do long before they had come within a few feet of us. When we got back to the academy, you showed me your hand, and his teeth marks were all over the knuckles of your right fist, which was bleeding. *Imagine his mouth*, you said. It wasn't Krav Maga, but the marks stayed there for weeks. Luisa noticed your hand at lunch a few days later and knew right away what had happened. The irony is that she didn't ask you; she asked me. At the time I believed no one suspected we were together. Turns out they all knew. She flew into a rage: *You could have gotten yourself killed, you could have been seriously hurt, they would have killed you and claimed it was self-defense.* None of these options had even crossed my mind. It occurs to me now that she would have fought them off, or at least stood between them and you.

This is another lesson in how much more she is suited to you. This woman would fight tooth and nail to save you. And to keep you. The fact that she was befriending me suddenly scared me. She must have assumed that I didn't matter, that I didn't stand a chance, that I was nothing. Just a fuck buddy.

Over time I grew to hate her solicitude and to dislike her, especially once it was clear that you and I had altogether stopped speaking, which is what she might have wanted, even without fully admitting it to herself. She did nothing to instigate our estrangement—she's not the type to—but I'm sure she noticed the chill creeping between former lovers who are condemned to have breakfast, lunch, and dinner in the same small dining room, to say nothing of our daily cocktail hour, and face each other every day with not a thing left to say and, worse yet, pretend that nothing significant ever existed between them. How two people can become strangers after what we had is totally beyond me. We've now even reached a point where we avoid glancing at each other. When I look, you're not looking; when you look, I look away. Why did we let this happen?

One night out of the blue, and without either of us planning it, we left the dining room at the same time. *Are you always going to ignore me?* I couldn't believe what I was hearing. *Don't you think we have the roles reversed? Reversed? How do you mean?* you asked. I hate when you do this. Then, also out of the blue: *There's a German film playing. And? Want to go?* I wanted to say yes right away, and I knew I was going to, but I also wanted to show that I was hesitating. *Sure, why not. Teresita is coming too.* I couldn't believe how I'd been ambushed. And so I spoke my mind. *I'd have gone with you alone. With Teresita you can go alone. She's a dancer. She'll make you happy. Still holding a grudge, then?* And suddenly I saw it as clear as day. *I'll always hold a grudge. Then you're not over me. Then I'm not over you.* I liked using your very words; it was like touching your lips, your mouth, and your forehead with my words. *Big surprise*, I added. I didn't mind telling you that I still cared, though it did hurt my pride, or what's left of it. *I'll tell her I changed my mind. Why, to go alone with me? Just go with her. OK, then*, you said. *I just thought the German film was the kind you'd like. Doesn't matter. Anyway, I've seen it already. But I'd still have gone with you*, I could have added. But I didn't.

When I returned to the dining room to make myself a quick cup of something warm instead of boiling it in my room, I ran into Luisa. She was seated at the head of the empty long table, which isn't her usual spot; no one was in the room, and she still hadn't gone home. She was drinking a chamomile tea. She looked a touch dejected. *What's wrong?* She smiled—one of those faraway, cordial smiles—then shook her head. *It's your turn to know.*

*Have you told him?*

*Never.*

Suddenly, from resenting her sweetness, I was filled with both awe and compassion for her. Here I am spilling my guts to you, and there she was watching you court one woman after the other. *Can I do anything to help?* She did not answer. *This helps,* she said, meaning my offer, or maybe just the chamomile. What a woman. I've never known so much patience mingled with such sorrow and fortitude in anyone before. Finally, standing up, she picked up her cup and saucer and went to place them in the kitchen. She put on her coat, which was sitting on the back of the chair next to her, and bade me good night. A few moments later I heard her car start.

Luisa is more in love with you than I thought.

More in love with you than I'll ever be.

This comforts me. But it also reminds me that maybe what I've been feeling all this time is hollow. A shallow form of hurt. Shallow love, lint love. It reminds me of those expensive cashmere sweaters found in luxury boutiques that are shimmering in their alluring dyes and the smoothest nap, but after being worn a few times are lined with lint and pills. Not the real deal at all. And maybe that's me: not the real deal. Which is why I lost you.

Sometimes I feel that life invited me to live. I accepted. But life changed its mind and gave me a rain check. Or maybe, without even knowing it, it was I who asked for the rain check, because I wanted more and better, and life had run out of options. *Come next year*, it said.

They said you left early this morning. You didn't say goodbye. They said it was urgent. I don't believe it. You probably used the word *urgent* so as not to upset the director, who hates people leaving before their term ends. I'm sure it won't be difficult to fill your spot with a wait-listed fellow, especially with Christmas just around the corner. I am planning to spend the holiday here; the place will most likely be quite deserted; they've already promised skimpy lunches and lighter fare for dinners, and the heat in one of the adjacent buildings will be turned off. Still, I'm looking forward to most of the fellows being gone, with very few of us left behind. Funny, I haven't spoken to you in quite a while, I try not to think of you that often, and yet your sudden disappearance revealed that I must have nursed some unspoken hopes that have now been dashed without my knowing exactly what they were. Perhaps a very tepid reconciliation or cautious détente that went no further than a perfunctory *You OK?* uttered on the stairwell—detached and stand-offish, yet nevertheless marked with the residual memory of something lost or locked away.

Now that's gone too.

After breakfast, I went up to your room, shut the door behind me, and stepped to the windows, where I stopped and rested my arms on the sill. Your space, your world, your view. Itamar. How strangely welcoming your room was now that you weren't there. This was the first time that I'd been to it without feeling rushed to leave. We only came here because you'd forgotten something, your wallet, your glasses, your cigarette contraption.

But I never had a chance to sit on one of your chairs or lie on your bed; besides, you always left your door open when we'd come in, as though you couldn't wait for us to get out. Only now could I see what your window overlooked: the train station, the gray thoroughfare, and the large dull fountain into which an installation artist had built a mad kennel in the shape of a cross. There was scant light in this room. I couldn't understand how they'd assign this room to a painter. I'd said so once. You said it wasn't important and let the matter drop.

Your bed was still unmade, and you'd left behind a cheap paperback copy of a spy novel on the floor. Fancy you reading spy novels—who'd have guessed.

In a few days, this room will belong to someone else and there won't be a trace of you. The old wooden hangers are lying on the floor by the old closet, scattered about like dead pigeons shot for practice and left for someone to clean up. That's so you. Someone would pick them up. So I picked them up myself. One by one, quietly, as though performing an act of penance for someone who couldn't be bothered. That's the sort of thing Luisa would do, pick up after you, as when she found your socks in the laundry room and folded each sock into its partner and then stacked each pair neatly. How did she know they were yours? Because she'd seen you wear them? No, because you're the only person at the academy who'd forget them in the laundry room and expect someone to bring them up to him neatly folded.

I found the last hanger on your bed, picked it up, and hung it with the others on the bar inside your closet. Had you forgotten anything? No. I still felt sorry for how dark your room could get—just a passing cloud and the light was gone. Yet you never complained. And then I remembered a week ago when I ran into you downstairs. You were chatting with the cook in the pantry and holding a paper bag containing two oatmeal cookies. *Would you share?* I interrupted. *Gladly.* You gave me a whole cookie. Then you sat on a stool and we began chatting. The usual jokes. The usual smile. Were we friends again? But I didn't dare ask. Why were you drawing in the coffee room? You liked it here. It's quiet, it's soothing. We spoke a bit more. You on the stool, with your knees parted, and me standing in front of you, almost like a supplicant myself now, holding a cookie I'd barely bitten because you kept making me laugh. You said you could get a third cookie if I wanted. Split in half? Split in half. You went back into the kitchen, clearly charmed the cook again, and were back in seconds with a cookie, which you proceeded to split in half. You gave me the larger half. *Why?* I asked. *Because. Because*, I repeated. Then, without preamble: *Would you come with me upstairs?* You were silent, your smile slackened. *The light is better*, I immediately added. *You can draw for as long as you like.* Why had I even attempted this? I knew it was pointless, and using light as an excuse, how unbelievably lame that was. I could tell I'd crossed a line the moment I opened my mouth and watched your face. And the strange thing is that it suddenly dawned on me that you knew I was going to ask something like that the moment you sat on the stool. So why did I ask? Because I'd never have been able to live with myself if I hadn't? Because I wanted you upstairs? Because I wanted you for me? Your answer came like a spike in a vampire's heart. *I don't think I can.*

How civil and forbearing your answer. And how

inexorably cruel. Were you testing me, or maybe even teasing, or were you as desperate as I was to deflect an awkward moment with the first thing that sprang into your head? *I don't think I can*, spoken with a resigned, near-melancholy inflection that implied authentic regret. It hurt because for once you were almost on the point of wishing you'd said yes and were sorry you couldn't.

Had we become such total strangers that I should catch myself blushing?

I let you have my half of the cookie, and was walking upstairs to my room when I stopped and turned around, clearly brewing cutting words, though I had no sense of what I'd say. Instead: *Will you ever forgive this awkward moment?*

*Forgiven and forgotten.* Spoken with your usual good-sport merriment while finishing my half of the oatmeal raisin cookie.

I wanted to apologize some more, but the apologies racing through my mind were so makeshift and flaccid that I kept quiet. If I had opened my mouth, I would most likely have said, *Can I ask you again?*

Had I said that, you would probably have said yes.

It would have been charity.

But then, even charity . . . *Forgiven and forgotten.* Those were the words I took to bed that night.

You'll never remember our brief exchange in the pantry.

Which is when it hit me: men had suddenly stopped looking at me. The older man at the train station, the barista, dear Robert, they felt sorry for me. Each one once but not more than once. Twice if I asked; I never asked. Men don't look at me when I wander beyond the compound of the academy. I'm the damaged dove. I can fly all right, and I coo and warble like the rest of them, but doves know I'm not to be mated with. They just know.

I'm the dove that stayed behind. Your empty room, that's me.

After deciding to take the spy novel with me and shutting the door to your room, I still didn't know whether what crushed me that afternoon in the pantry was your blunt refusal or the embarrassment of having misread our breezy banter for a resurgence of warmth between us. The part that hurt most, however, was not so much your refusal but knowing I had definitely lost you the moment I'd asked you to come upstairs. The two are the same, I know, but they are staggered, first the blow to the face, then the knife in the gut.

I should never have spoken.

I should have said something else, but I didn't. After that day I had no more masks to wear. You continued to say hello to me because I didn't mean anything; I couldn't because you meant the world still.

No one heard from you until we received a postcard from Paris. I found myself examining the postmark because I couldn't believe anything any longer. The trouble is that, now that I am trying to recall our time together, you never really lied. You were, at worst, cagey and evasive. You just didn't want to see me hurt. So you skimmed the truth.

Oh, well. Forgiven!

I knew you never loved me. Just as I sometimes think I never loved you, even at the beginning. Perhaps I didn't want to admit this to myself, just as there's a part of me still unwilling to think that I did love you. There was always something like denial or even distaste woven into every thought of you, but once you said, *I don't think I can*, all I desperately wanted was you, perhaps because you'd finally shut the door on me and I knew it would never be reopened. When I did open it, you had already left. Perhaps I went in there to prove everyone wrong, almost hoping to catch you still there, sleeping, or lying in bed reading your spy novel. It was like walking into someone's room the morning after they'd died and hoping to find them still there, drinking their coffee in bed. Only two days before he died, I'd been rubbing my grandfather's shoulders with cream. Only last month you and I were in this room to pick up the cell phone you'd forgotten on your nightstand. Now the room contains just lifeless hangers without purpose.

Ironically, now that you're gone for good, I can no longer pretend that I don't miss you.

Can I even imagine what life will be like after you're gone? What will my last remaining Sundays be without hoping to run into you—those desperate, last-minute errands to buy groceries on moribund Sundays, my last card before darkness sets in? I go to bed each night thinking of you, wake up still thinking of you; sometimes I try not to shut an eye because I don't want to stop thinking of you, and would welcome nightmares if you promised to be in them. All I want is to be in your arms. No sex if that's not what you want, no kissing if my lips don't turn you on, maybe both of us fully clothed, you in dungarees, me in my faded sweats and my shirt totally buttoned up this time, just being in your arms, just hugging, falling asleep together. If someone else were writing these words, I'd say they were fooling themselves. Yet all I want is to be in your arms as I was when we made love. Yes, I dared call it making love because it was your way, inherited from your mother in who knows what nameless village in Itamarland where children run wild on bare feet and rush home to their mothers when they summon them for a wonderful meal, a hug, another hug, and one more, my love, 'cause I missed you as I know you missed me. Itamarlove. You could have been totally indifferent to me, yet you'd have stared at me as if you were famished for what I had to offer, and both your hunger and your gratitude sat in your dark eyes when you looked at me that way, and I couldn't tell if this was love or something just like it, or simply your way of saying, *Thanks, you're wonderful, Mariana.*

You're with me now, as I write to you—and I don't want to stop writing. Every night I write here. And it is like being with you. I complain, I moan, I bicker, and I blame. You never reply, you hear me out, you nod. You've been with me all this time. Sometimes I take my laptop to bed and I'm in bed with you. Every night I write here. You listen, you nod, just nodding is good enough.

A friend tells me not to send this letter, to write it for myself and then to put it away. But that would be like chewing on a cake filled with custard, currants, and candied fruit drawn from the most exotic spots only to refuse to swallow, like drinking the best wines and doing as wine buffs do, spitting the wine in a beaker. If I write my letter it's for you to read.

But I'm lying. I'll never have the guts to send it. So why write? To be with you? To jostle you? To bother you? I don't know.

Maybe it's not even to spite you or hurt you, but to put you in the shoes of someone who loved you so passionately that it's possibly through shame, not empathy or pity, that you'll finally understand, and by understanding learn to regret what I was so ready to offer. But isn't this the ultimate illusion: hoping that one day the person who booted me out of his life will, by reading what I've put to paper, realize, but only when it's too late, that what I had to give, what was simply there for the taking, was precisely what he hungered for most and would gladly have traded all his fleeting Wendys, Elisas, Ekaterinas for? But here is the cruel irony: I may have been right to offer what I had, I was just the wrong donor.

So here I am lying in my bed with my laptop sitting on my blanket, and rather than write about an obscure novel published in 1669, all I want to do is think of you. I do so in spurts, thank goodness. First, my mind drifts to other things, then something hurts, then you're here, and all I do is write to you, talk to you, try as best I can to resurrect memories of our brief time together. There are days when I still expect a card from you. I like expecting a sign that I know won't come. There's a young Slovenian composer in our midst who receives thick airmail envelopes every few days. He pores over them, and you can't even speak to him while he's reading. His mother, his girlfriend, his partner, who knows. I envy him. I wish you'd send me a thick-wadded envelope so that I too could sink into one of those totally sagging armchairs in the coffee room and read something that I know won't be an apology, or a reconciliation, or even an invitation to join you wherever you are at this moment. I'll accept the most perfunctory card, an email, a text. All I want is contact, even if you feel obliged to remind me there's never going to be anything between us. I want contact the way all I wanted on that one fateful afternoon when you turned me down was contact. Just to lie down together and be held, it's all I want, I promise.

In one month, one year, who will I be, how will I look back on all this? Will I still ache, will I still want to ache, will there be someone new, or will I look back on this one season in hell and say I was better off then than I am today, I was alive at the time, now what am I?

I know I'll never send this letter. But I won't throw it away. If I have a son, I want him to find it one day and see your name and wonder who this Itamar was. I want him to look you up or write, saying, *Mariana died. I found your name among her things and wanted to let you know.* Why would he need to let you know? Because nothing ends. If you too are dead, maybe my son will track down your children and tell them *I found this about your father, I thought you might want a copy. I'd love to meet you.* I can just see our adult children humoring one another, wondering who I was and who you were that year, only to cap everything with a resigned and simple *Poor souls, it was so long ago.* And indeed, it already feels so very long ago, though you've barely left, and yet all I need is to hear the wind slam the door downstairs to catch myself suddenly doing something I can't fight against and don't want to unlearn: to hope it's you. And now that I think of it, the one thing that still can't die even after the two of us have died is this very hope. It's stirred back up the moment the door slams, the moment I hear footfalls up the stairs followed by the one or two accidental chimes of your bicycle bell, until the door opens and I slip both arms under your unbuttoned thick wool coat and won't let go. Now, that could never, must never, die. It gets passed on to someone else. I envy our heirs.

# Postface

I wanted to write *Mariana* many years ago, during one of the hottest summers ever known. In June and July of that year I spent entire days sitting on the rooftop of a building in Cambridge, Massachusetts, reading works written during the reign of Louis XIV. I had my small radio tuned to a classical program; I was wearing a bathing suit, a loose shirt, sunglasses, a hat, and sunblock. Periodically, and as described in my novel *Harvard Square*, I would step down one flight to my small apartment to refill a glass of cold water. There were two other sunbathers on the roof, all three of us preparing for our oral exams and dissertations. We would occasionally speak, then return to our work: no distractions allowed. Later, in the afternoon, I would be drinking a lemonade spiked with a bit of gin. Sometimes I'd offer the other two a glass as well; they'd accept, but not always. I read the memoirs of the Cardinal de Retz, long selections from Saint-Simon, everything by Madame de La Fayette, Racine, Pascal, La Rochefoucauld, and Pierre Nicole. But the one work that transfixed me was *The Portuguese Letters*, a very slim volume of five letters allegedly written by a slighted young Portuguese nun to the French officer who returned to France after seducing and forsaking her. Her name, which she reveals twice in her letters, is Mariana. I fell in love with her voice.

I wanted to tell her story again. But I did not dare. The desire to do so was renewed when I assigned the work before the pandemic in my graduate seminar and decided to reread it for the nth time. I was no less transfixed this time. The candor of Mariana's sorrow, the polish and tact of her resolve to purge her letters of all bitterness, and the irresistible grace of her wisdom when she pleads with her lover but already knows it's to no avail, all these won me over. I was in awe of her disenchanted, almost ruthless insights into her lover, but her insights into herself were no less ruthless. The French call this disabused raw mindset *ésprit de pénétration*. The summer after my course I decided to write a modern version about a graduate student called Mariana.

She is in her early twenties and is spending time in an academy in Italy while working on a manuscript about a novel published in 1669. The situation is quite similar to that of *Call Me by Your Name*, except that this time it is not Oliver, but Mariana, and she is hosted not in the home of a professor but in an academy. I had several spots in Italy in mind for the academy, but I did not name it. On her first evening, during an orientation cocktail party, Mariana meets an artist staying at the same academy and is immediately struck by him. Their attraction is instantaneous and passionate, and all of her traditional, Midwestern American safeguards are instantly shoved aside. The girl is totally smitten. The man's passion cools soon enough.

It is impossible to think of anyone who has not confronted rejection at least once in life or not been made to feel dejected by a beloved's cold shoulder. Who hasn't obsessed over the comings and goings of a long-lost lover, of someone we once held in our arms and who now haunts all our thoughts but wants nothing to do with us? Who of us hasn't been heartbroken when unable to speak with someone we still desire but who has hardly set eyes on us? When we see that person, our words die in our mouths. The only one who could comfort us is the very one who causes our grief.

Set as a letter she may never decide to send, my Mariana's narrative is about two things: the remembrance of her torrid affair and her regrets over her fruitless attempts to win her lover back. In the interim Mariana realizes that this man has almost always lied to her and cheated on her. The only person she respects now is the secretary of the academy, who is resigned to nurse her undisclosed love for the same man; he will never know of her love, much less pay her any mind. Mariana envies the secretary's silent forbearance. But she herself is incapable of it. One night when she runs into the man in the academy's kitchen, she can't help but ask him to her room. His answer surprises her.

Written not by a woman but by a French diplomat named Gabriel-Joseph de Lavergne, comte de Guilleragues (1628–1684), the original tale of Mariana became the rage of French society in 1669. Her five letters were soon followed by more letters penned by different writers, some claiming to be by the same distraught nun, others by the French officer who was answering her first batch of letters, followed by more and more letters yet. There were several collections of "Portuguese letters" around Europe, and by today's standards these could easily fall in the realm of fan fiction.

Mariana Alcoforado (1640–1723), who was later presumed to be the author of the letters, was indeed a Portuguese novitiate, but it is doubtful that she was the Mariana of the letters. Still today, though, in Portugal and Brazil, Mariana Alcoforado retains pride of place as the author of the letters. Ironically, the Portuguese "original" of *The Portuguese Letters* was never found, or, what is more likely, never even existed, which explains why the version that is normally accepted as authentic in the Portuguese-speaking world is none other than one translated from the French.

The fate of the beguiled and smitten Mariana might explain why readers were so taken by the mere mention of a young nun allowing her French lover into her tiny cell—this not only at great risk to her reputation, her family, and the honor of her cloister but also to herself, since the penalty for any relationship with a man was exceptionally severe. One can assume that her forbidden love for the officer might have drawn many readers eager to picture the licentious scene in her cell, but Guilleragues details none of it. Mariana is alone.

One is always alone after the end of love. And maybe this is what I wanted to capture in my version of Mariana's tale—not just the pain of watching someone's love, if love it ever was, turn its back on her, but also the loneliness that follows in the wake of love, loneliness we believed expunged once and for all from our lives but that is suddenly thrust back by the very person who, for a short while, seemed to have apparently rescued us from it. This, in the end, is what we find difficult to forgive. Not that we were deceived, but that we brought this deceit upon ourselves, fed on it, let it fester, and needed it at any cost, because without it we'd be back to being who we know we are: unloved, undone, and alone.